PUFFIN BOOKS

X MARKS THE SPOT

'X marks the spot,' said Cop – but he was too badly
injured in the helicopter crash to tell Peter, Louise and
Ross more than this. So they have to find X for themselves, which isn't easy, for they not only haven't a clue
what X is, but they have crashed in the middle of the
New Zealand bush, with no maps and very little equipment. Making their way through the forest and living
off the land are not their only problems though, for other
people are after the mysterious X too; the dangerous,
unscrupulous characters who sabotaged the helicopter . . .

Joan de Hamel's story is a real thriller, full of high
tension and unexpected twists. A first-rate adventure
story for readers of ten and over.

D1392993

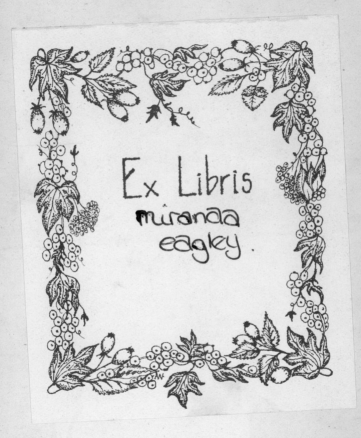

Ex Libris
miranda
eagley.

JOAN DE HAMEL

X MARKS THE SPOT

PUFFIN BOOKS

Puffin Books, Penguin Books Ltd, Harmondsworth, Middlesex, England
Penguin Books, 40 West 23rd Street, New York, New York 10010, U.S.A.
Penguin Books Australia Ltd, Ringwood, Victoria, Australia
Penguin Books Canada Ltd, 2801 John Street, Markham, Ontario, Canada L3R 1B4
Penguin Books (N.Z.) Ltd, 182–190 Wairau Road, Auckland 10, New Zealand

—

First published by Lutterworth Press 1973
Published in Puffin Books 1976
Reprinted 1980, 1984

—

Text and illustrations copyright © Joan de Hamel, 1973
All rights reserved

—

Made and printed in Great Britain
by Richard Clay (The Chaucer Press), Ltd
Bungay, Suffolk
Set in Linotype Baskerville

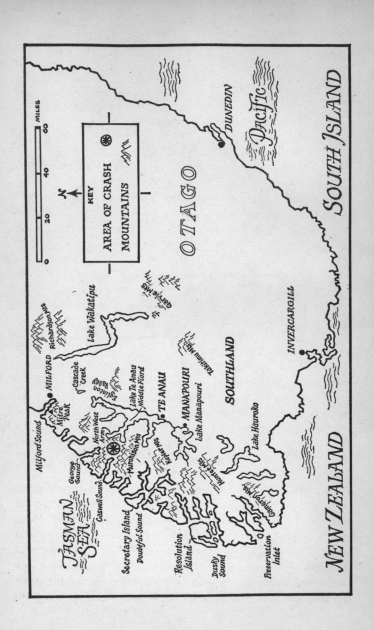

CHAPTER ONE

'BIT of a mist rising,' shouted Peter, from his seat next to his uncle in the helicopter.

The mountains ahead of them had scarves of cloud at about a thousand feet, where the deep bush thinned out into snow-grass. In the valleys the mist was becoming dense.

'All the better in some ways,' Cop shouted back, his right hand holding the cyclic stick, his left resting on the throttle. He seemed about to say something else, but apparently changed his mind. It was an effort to make oneself heard above the noise of the engine.

The helicopter was flying steadily away from Te Anau in a nor-westerly direction. Peter, sitting in the middle seat, had the dual control levers in front of him. Sometimes when he flew with his uncle, Cop would let him take over one control, perhaps the collective lever or the pedals, while Cop kept the helicopter correctly balanced with the other three controls. Not a chance of practising on this trip, though. Not with the family aboard. Peter glanced at the altimeter. Cop was keeping very low, in spite of the mist. Peter wondered why.

So did Lou, the eldest of the three children. She was on Peter's right in the third seat and she was not a bit comfortable because the youngest member of the family, Ross, was sprawled awkwardly on top of her, trying to pretend he was not actually sitting on anyone's lap. The same seat belt enclosed them both. It is not convenient to take one adult and three children in a helicopter designed for three adults, but it is not impossible. It was worth putting up

7

with the discomfort for the wonderful holiday that lay ahead of them.

Lou did wish, though, that Cop would keep higher above the trees and further out of the mist. She hoped that where they were going, beyond the mountains, down on the seaward side, the Tasman breezes would have blown the mist away from the Sounds. She hoped especially that their little bay at Dolphin Sound would be clear, where the holiday cottage waited to welcome them.

Ross's day-dreams were very different. He imagined them coming in to an almost blind landing, Cop having trouble with the controls and relying entirely on Ross's sharp eyesight and faultless sense of direction. Actually Ross too wondered why Cop was flying so low, but there was probably some good reason and he did not want to show his ignorance by asking. Peter knew the 'chopper' and its habits from nose to tail. But Ross, two years younger, had only been included on occasional trips. Lou had never flown in it before. Ross sensed she was scared and was glad she at least had the tact to keep her mouth shut and not make a public nuisance of herself.

Now Cop was leaning sideways, peering down through the transparent door on his side of the cockpit.

'Neat little hanging valley down there,' he shouted.

The children looked down. The bush opened up into a sort of semi-circle of tussock grass.

'Mind if we land for half an hour and have a look-see?' asked Cop, at the top of his voice.

'Fine,' shouted Peter, thumbs up.

The helicopter hovered above the valley but kept beneath the wisps of mist that curled among the rocky tops of the main divide. The snow-grass up there was thinly spread over the crags, like a threadbare cloak. Further down the bush looked like a solid green quilted cushion. One would never have known, seeing it from the air, that the biggest trees were up to sixty feet high and that between the leaf canopy and the earth was a dense tangle of

8

trees of every size and age. They sprawled, one over another, clambering for a place in the sun, choked by even more determined creepers, festooned with mosses, overrun by ferns and fungi, struggling out of the dark morass of rotting vegetation and leaf-mould down below.

There was just this one place where a helicopter could land, this curve of tussock at the foot of the cliff. A white streak, which was a waterfall, looked like a trickle of whitewash running down the cliff-side. Further down the valley there was an occasional glint of water, showing the direction in which the creek flowed, but the gathering mist blotted out the lower reaches.

Peter was again asking himself *why*. Cop seemed to have something on his mind. Ross was not bothered. He was dead keen on any form of adventure or exploring. Lou was deciding that coming down in a helicopter was even worse than going up. She felt so exposed in the plastic bubble of the cockpit, swinging in mid-air, suspended by nothing. It was obvious that the slightest miscalculation would plunge the rotor arms into the tangle of the bush or shear them clean off against that awful cliff. She did feel terribly sick — If only Ross would sit still instead of bouncing about against her stomach as he peered eagerly this way and that.

Very gracefully, delicately, the helicopter alighted on the tussock, like a gnat on the surface of a pond. The ski-like skids gently took the weight as Cop reduced the throttle to nothing, turned off the fuel. The engine vibrations stopped. They were firmly on the ground, although the rotor arm continued to swing round and round in seemingly perpetual motion.

After the roaring which had deafened them in flight, the noise of the waterfall seemed no more than the distant pulse of the silent bush.

Ross was scrabbling at the seat belt, eager to get out.

'Watch it!' said Cop, opening the door on his side.

'Don't want this chopper to chop off any heads, so mind that rotor.'

Ross wriggled out, bent almost double, and scampered clear. Lou and Peter followed with care. There was something sinister about the swish of that rotating arm, turning and turning so needlessly, on and on.

Cop was already passing round a tube of Poof anti-sandfly cream, and they all hastily rubbed it over their skin as the tiny black flies began to gather for a feast.

'Beastly things,' grumbled Ross, swiping a few dare-devils which had reached the back of his neck before the ointment had, 'what do they eat when *we* aren't here?'

'Starve,' said Peter, 'that's why they're so hungry.'

Ross grunted.

'I see – relief for the starving millions, is it? Give your blood and all that.'

Lou still felt sick. She sat down, holding her stomach. To her surprise Cop came and sat beside her. He seemed a little ill at ease.

'Come here, would you, Peter and Ross, before you start exploring – I want to explain something.' His tone of voice surprised the boys. Cop was usually so happy-go-lucky. Now suddenly he sounded serious.

'You see,' went on Cop, as they gathered round, 'this isn't going to be the sort of holiday that's all lounging around and lolling in the sun. I've got some work to do. And I want your help. It's something secret.'

'What do you mean?' asked Lou. 'Aren't we going to the cottage after all?' She had been looking forward so much to the cottage.

Ross felt a delicious tingle of adventure. Peter just said, 'Out with it, please, Cop.'

'We-ll,' said Cop, 'I've been asked to ... shall I say ... reconnoitre a certain area of dense bush between Te Anau and our cottage for a very special reason. A very secret reason actually. But I feel it's only fair to tell you that you're already in on it, whether you like it or not, because you three give me the perfect excuse to stay in this area. On the surface it's all joy-rides, excursions, the usual holiday picnics. But it'll be with an ulterior motive. Don't worry, Lou,' Cop added with a smile, 'it's all perfectly innocent.'

Lou looked bewildered. Peter frowned.

'Aren't you going to share the secret? Tell us what we're looking for?'

'Sorry, Peter,' said Cop, 'that's a bit hush. Not really my story to tell. Let's say we're looking for ... possums, shall we? Possum holes, droppings, nibbled tree-ferns, that sort of thing. But your help comes chiefly from giving me the excuse to go messing around exploring spots like this.'

The practical Peter was far from satisfied but Ross was not concerned. His philosophy was action first and questions later.

Lou could not believe her ears. Here they were, an ordinary New Zealand family, off on an ordinary summer Christmas holiday, and now Cop was talking about secrets and special reasons – and it was plain that possums had nothing to do with it at all. Possums were pests. They even came into town gardens and nibbled off buds and scared town-dwellers by thundering over the corrugated-iron roofs of the houses with a noise like a cattle stampede. On second thoughts, perhaps this holiday was not exactly run-of-the-mill. Not everyone's uncle had a helicopter. But lots of people went for holidays by air and lots of people had cottages down by the Southern Lakes. Not so many in the Sounds, where the bush is still not fully explored and mapped. But people went to Milford and Cascade Creek and along the Eglinton and Hollyford Valleys. Everything so far had seemed quite normal and their father and mother had agreed enthusiastically that the children should go to the cottage with Cop straight after Christmas. Their father was working till mid-January and then Cop was going to fetch him and Mother so they all had the last fortnight of the holidays together at Dolphin Sound.

'Do Dad and Mum know?' she asked. 'That there's a secret?'

'Oh yes,' said Cop, 'they know it's nothing sinister. It's my guess your father's put two and two together. Maybe you will too. It's just that I'm not telling because I promised not to. That's all.'

'What do you want us to do here?' asked Lou, still hankering to get on to the cottage and looking bleakly round the rock-strewn valley.

'Just a quick look-see,' said Cop, 'while this mist keeps out prying eyes. We'll just spend half an hour snooping, and if it's hopeful come back another day for a so-called picnic and explore more thoroughly.'

'Oh!' said Lou.

Cop gave her a big grin.

'You look as though your stomach hasn't caught up with you yet. You stay right here, Lou, while the boys and I look around under the cliff near the waterfall.'

Lou nodded. She was glad to sit still for a bit longer. The boys and Cop went tearing off. For a minute or so Lou watched the rotor arm, now only just turning; each circle seemed as if it must be the last, but she counted ten more before it finally came to rest. The helicopter's skids were loaded with gear. Cop had flown in stores and fuel to the cottage the previous week, but their packs were on the skids, with sleeping-bags, tent and last-minute bits and pieces. Cop always carried emergency rations when he flew and his rifle was always fixed below the seats, across the pockets containing maps and first aid kit. These, together with an axe and fire extinguisher, were part of the routine equipment of the machine.

Lou got up slowly and walked along the side of the creek for a few yards until she came to where the bush grew almost to the water's edge. It was dim and green in the bush; there was the special sweet damp smell of wet leaves and unseen flowers. Lou remembered being told that the rain forests in West Africa were like this, except, of course, that there were no jungle animals here in New Zealand, only birds and insects and some deer and ... possums. Possums. Why should Cop want possums?

Lou sat down on a fallen tree and then, to reassure herself, took a pencil and note-book from the breast pocket of her woollen bush shirt. Lou liked to draw. It was more than 'like'; she *needed* to draw. She drew when she was happy, to make the moment permanent; she drew when she was bored and when she was sad, to escape from the situation and view it, as it were, from the outside. So now she began to sketch the first thing she noticed, a fern that grew from a crack in the tree-stump. With fine spindly strokes she wiggled away at the outline, counting the ins and outs, wondering whether the brown dots were spores or seeds. 'Are ferns fungi or plants?' she mused. She would look them up later. The first thing was to make a drawing and jot down the colours.

Soon her page was damp with fine spray from the waterfall. She was conscious now of its roar as it leapt like a foaming monster down the cliff and then turned back into a modest, docile creek as soon as it had recovered from its heroics. She could not draw a waterfall, but she looked at the tree-ferns scrambling one over another to take advantage of the black moist earth. She began to draw a tree-fern. Then a bush robin came down to see her and perched on a stone near her feet. She left the tree-fern unfinished and tried to draw the bird instead, but it kept bobbing and flicking its tail and hopping back and forth, giving a thin squeaking call ...

'Birds are terribly fidgety,' thought Lou, trying to finish its back view from memory, without success. She jotted *bush robin* by her effort and at that moment a black-and-white male tomtit flitted on to a branch and the 'bush robin' flew up to join it. Lou had to laugh at herself. Bush robin! It was a female tomtit; the same yellow-brown as a bush robin but much smaller, with white on the wing, like its husband. She tried to write down the call note – *Tsts wee*. Really, birds were difficult; couldn't they even say anything original?

Cop and Peter and Ross were coming back towards her. Ross was chattering about a shallow cave they had found, almost under the waterfall, Peter carrying a half-

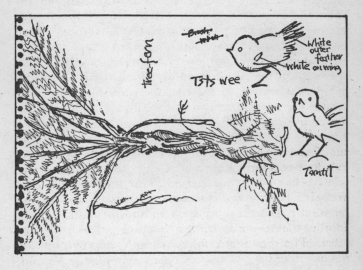

demolished tree-fern and explaining rather loudly that possums always ate tree-fern fronds like that. Cop said, 'Yes, yes,' but he was not sure that those were possum droppings that they had seen. He seemed more interested in *not*-possums than possums.

Lou snapped her note-book shut and stood up. She felt absolutely all right again and longing to go on to the cottage.

'All right, then,' said Cop. 'All aboard. I think we might call here again one day, but now the next stop is the cottage in time for tea.'

They clambered back into the cockpit and fastened

their seat belts. Cop switched on, checked the dials; he pressed the red starter button below the throttle handle. Inside the cockpit they felt the engine vibrations and were deafened by the noise; outside the tussock grass and the near-by trees seemed to flinch from the sound waves, were flattened by the turbulence from the whizzing rotor.

Cop twisted the throttle, the roar increased, he adjusted the tail rotor, easing the cyclic stick and bracing his feet against the left pedal that controlled the rear rotor and the steering. The helicopter rose vertically.

At about thirty feet everything happened at once. Ross's sharp eyes saw something fly off and bounce into the grass. Lou was conscious of the whole machine spinning round and there was a terrific roar as the engine revved uselessly. Peter turned to see black exhaust smoke billowing out below the petrol tanks. Then the engine cut – everyone seemed to be sitting on air, like astronauts in a state of weightlessness, straining upwards against the safety belts that anchored them to their seats, They were dropping, the ground hit them; crash, it was over. No, the rebound jerked them up again and down, another crash, another bounce, crash for the third time. The helicopter subsided on the tussock, flat on its belly, the skids splayed out on either side. The rotor blade went round and round, silently, ceaselessly, round and round and round.

CHAPTER TWO

WHAT on earth had happened? Peter could not grasp the situation at all. One minute everything fine, and now chaos. What were they meant to do now?

Peter turned to Cop. Cop sat quite still, his head drooping, both arms hanging loosely. No help from Cop.

'Well, I suppose it's over to me then,' thought Peter slowly. 'I suppose we ought to get out.'

On his other side Ross, sprawled across Lou, was making the most horrible choking noises. Peter, fumbling, unclicked his own safety belt, leant over and unfastened the one across Lou and Ross. Then he wrenched open the door beyond them.

'Get out! Get out!' he heard himself saying over and over again. 'And mind your heads.'

Ross had already stopped the worst of the choking noises – he had been squeezed across the chest so tightly by the strain on the belt that he could not get his breath. Peter gave him a push and Ross tumbled wheezing on to the tussock.

'Get out, Lou!' shouted Peter, wondering hazily why everyone was being so slow and stupid.

Lou just sat. Thousands of dreams and flashes and space rockets and high-speed drills gyrated and vibrated somewhere behind her eyes. Voices were shouting her name but she could not answer. After that there was a gap and she woke up desperately thirsty, and then Peter was leaning over her as she lay on the grass; he said, 'Knocked out cold, but you're fine now, Lou; don't worry.'

'Water,' said Lou, so Peter went to the creek. He was

suddenly thirsty himself and plunged his head into the water, gulped down big mouthfuls and came up feeling much more himself. He scooped up water in his hands and ran back quickly to Lou, opened his fingers and poured it into her mouth.

Lou watched him go for some more and just then Ross's face appeared and he croaked:

'Gee, I'm sorry, Lou, it was my head. My head got you on the corner of your jaw. I knocked you out. And I got squeezed by the belt.'

Peter emptied another scoop of water over Lou's face and then crept round the nose of the helicopter, keeping his head well down. For a moment he braced himself for what he might see when he opened the door next to Cop.

Cop was slouching forwards, held by his safety belt which looked rather slack. His hands, hanging between his knees, had blood trickling down the fingers on to the floor. Peter began to feel sick. He peered up into his uncle's face. It was hard to see it; Cop was slumped so low that his face was in shadow. A cut on his chin was bleeding freely, the blood dripping on to his hands below. Not a bad cut, though. Peter noticed the smell of citronella and saw a broken glass bottle of liquid Poof on the floor. That would account for the cut, but Cop's eyes were shut, his face was pale and somehow unreal ...

'Cop!' yelled Peter. 'Hey! Wake up, Cop!'

Cop did not move. But he began to mutter, 'Don't touch me; my back, great pain.'

'But, Cop,' cried Peter, 'can't you get out? I mean, suppose ...' Suddenly he realized what had been at the back of his mind all the time. 'The petrol, Cop, high octane – it could catch fire.'

'Others out,' said Cop indistinctly.

Peter did not know whether that was a question or an order.

'Yes, the others are all fine, all safe. It's just you, Cop.'

17

'Thank God!' whispered Cop.

'Can I radio for help? What shall I do?' went on Peter.

'Out of range,' said Cop. 'Just give me a little time. Don't move me. Fire extinguisher.'

Peter had forgotten that. He reached carefully under Cop's legs and unclipped it. He wondered whether to use it on the petrol tanks, just in case, but decided to keep it for an emergency and laid it carefully on the grass. He thought he had better stay close to the chopper and watch till he was certain the fire risk was over.

He flopped on the grass. He still felt very peculiar himself. Literally shaken up. He kept thinking, 'Thank heavens our safety belts were tight or we'd all be dead.' Then slowly he remembered how slack Cop's belt had looked and began to wonder what those crashes and rebounds would have done to someone who was not securely anchored.

'Terrific jerks,' Peter remembered, 'give anyone's bottom a fearful bashing I should think; wham against the seat each time on the rebounds.'

Ross stood up, tested his arms and legs, and finding all in working order and his breathing almost back to normal, walked over to Peter and squatted down beside him.

'What's wrong with Cop?' he asked, still rather husky-voiced. 'Can't he get out? Is he dead, Peter?'

'He's alive.' Peter tried not to sound too worried. 'But he says he wants to stay where he is for the moment. Hurt his back a bit. I say, Ross,' he added to change the subject, 'I'm all in a muddle. It happened so quickly. Why on earth did the chopper go and do that?'

Ross suddenly remembered what he'd seen.

'A bit fell off,' he announced.

Peter stared. 'Are you certain, Ross?'

'Positive,' said Ross, 'I noticed. It fell over there.'

He pointed, and began to walk towards the cliff. Peter heaved himself up and scrambled after him and caught up just as Ross cried, 'There it is!' and bent to pick up a stick-like object about eighteen inches long with a knob at each end.

'Don't touch it!' cried Peter. 'Watch out, it could be hot.'

Ross stepped back and they both stared at the rod. The knobs were made of leather, gathered round the rod like the business end of a drumstick.

'That's the bit that joins the engine to the long shaft,' said Peter slowly, 'I'm pretty certain. The short shaft, I think it's called.'

'If that's the short shaft, what's the long shaft?' asked Ross. He did not usually ask Peter for information, Peter was so tiresomely know-all, but he just had to find out this time and there was no one else to ask.

Peter led Ross back to the helicopter. 'It goes right down the spine of this tail bit,' he explained, 'something like the mainshaft in a car. The engine turns one end and the other end makes the tail rotor spin. Of course, when this bit dropped off – see, there's the gap – the engine was turning nothing except the main rotor arm and that's why it revved so violently. And all that exhaust. And why we spun round. No steering.'

'What I want to know,' said Ross stubbornly, 'is why it dropped off. I mean, bits don't drop off things for nothing.'

'No,' said Peter, 'not with the maintenance Cop gives this chopper.'

'If you see what I mean,' persisted Ross.

'Too right I do,' said Peter. Perhaps it was because Cop had been talking about secrets but Peter certainly shared Ross's suspicions.

'Could've been tampered with,' he found himself saying.

'To make us crash.' Ross was both horrified and delighted.

Suddenly Cop's voice, quiet but steady, came from the helicopter cockpit.

'Peter, Ross, come here.' It was a command. The boys obeyed at once.

Cop's chin had stopped bleeding but his face still looked terrible, with his mouth stretched in a way that told of great pain: also of great anxiety.

'I heard you,' said Cop quietly. 'Fetch the short shaft. It won't be hot.'

Ross ran off and Peter began to ask Cop how he was, but Cop brushed aside the questions with 'Not now, later.' When Ross came back Cop moved his hand with care and took the short shaft. Slowly he examined one knob: then the other. 'I checked this myself,' was all he said.

'So someone's interfered with it?' asked Peter.

'Yes,' said Cop, and his voice had lost its strength. He seemed unable to focus his eyes any longer, but he clutched the short shaft, his knuckles pale. 'A drink,' he muttered.

Ross ran off again. He had found a billy somewhere and was soon helping Cop drink. Then Cop's head slumped back and he shut his eyes.

'Well,' said Peter after a long silence, 'we'd better see if Lou's all right.'

As he stepped back from the helicopter he found he did not know what to do about anything. He wandered to the creek and had another long drink. He could not even remember what he ought to be thinking about. Then he stumbled towards Lou. His legs gave way underneath him.

'Come on,' cried Ross, who seemed as resilient as ever, 'let's get the gear off the skids. Gee! just look at those skids. The poor old chopper looks like a squashed spider with legs in all directions.'

To Peter's enormous relief Lou stood up.

'I'll help Ross,' she whispered gently to Peter. 'I think I'm over the worst. In fact, I've been asleep. It's your turn for a spell. It's shock, I think; I've read about it. It sort of hits you after an accident. Have a rest.'

Together Lou and Ross tugged at the smashed remains

20

of their belongings. The sleeping-bags were all right and the tent and clothes, which were rolled up and tied inside a blanket. The packs and a box of stores were scattered far and wide. Ross collected up bits of the pie that their mother had made for the first evening meal. There was a tin of instant coffee, bashed in but intact, a packet of freeze-dried peas and a plastic bag of crumbs that had once been home-made biscuits. Lou and Ross piled all the salvage near Peter, who seemed to be asleep.

'Are there any matches anywhere?' asked Lou. 'We need a camp fire and a billy of water on the boil to make coffee. A hot drink would do us all good.'

'I've got matches,' cried Ross proudly, and at that moment Peter suddenly woke up. The word 'matches' had penetrated his confused dreams.

'No!' he shouted, so suddenly and loudly that Lou thought he must be out of his mind. She put on a maternal sort of voice, which always maddened her brothers.

'It's all right, Peter, go back to sleep. We'll have a lovely fire going in no time and you'll soon be right with a nice drink of coffee and some food.'

'No!' shouted Peter again. 'The petrol; it's high octane. The smallest spark'd blow the tanks sky-high. And Cop with them. Even the heat from a fire could do it.'

Lou gasped. 'Oh, gosh!' she said. 'Oh, gosh! I'm not thinking straight. I ought to 've thought of that.'

Peter took a deep breath. 'Listen, both of you,' he said, 'we've all had a bashing. None of us is thinking straight. I bet we're not, even if we think we are,' he went on quickly, to interrupt Ross's protests, 'and it's getting late. Let's eat what we can find, get the tent up, pile inside it and go to sleep. And hope we're more intelligent by morning.'

'Some hope,' grumbled Ross. 'Anyway, that's what we were going to do, Lou and I'd already decided . . .' He did not mention the fire; the petrol risk had not occurred to him either. But Peter was always telling people what to do

21

when they knew already and Ross always resented being bossed.

Somehow all three of them worked for another half hour. Something had to be done with Cop. They spoke to him but he did not answer. Very carefully they undid his seat belt and lifted his legs across the other seats and rolled up a blanket to make a pillow to support his head. They put his sleeping-bag across him for warmth. He groaned and muttered and clutched the short shaft as though it helped him bear the pain.

Then, munching bits of pie and crumbly biscuit, the children put up the tent near the helicopter so they could hear if Cop called in the night. Outside the tent Lou put some things she thought they might need: a torch, a billy of water and a beaker, the fire extinguisher. Then she crawled into the tent and down her sleeping-bag. The boys were already curled up.

Lou tried to say her prayers, conscious of an enormous 'thank you' that needed to be said, but before she could think of any words she, like her brothers, had fallen asleep.

In the darkest, coldest hour of the night, Lou woke up. Cop was saying something.

Lou scrambled out of her sleeping-bag and ran across to him. The grass was wet and freezing cold. She had grabbed the torch, was able to get up into the cockpit beside him, and flashed the light for a moment on his face. His eyes were open; the blood had congealed on his chin.

'Cop! It's me, Lou; you all right?'

'Drink,' said Cop.

Lou left the torch on the floor and ran to fetch a beaker-ful of water. Back to Cop, shivering with cold so that she slopped some of the water out of the beaker. She helped him drink.

'Cop, where are you hurt? Can I make you more comfortable?'

'Think I must have cracked something in my back,' said Cop, 'hurts like hell to try and move my legs. Top half's all right.'

'For heaven's sake keep your legs still,' cried Lou, 'we'll get help somehow.'

'Yes,' said Cop, 'that's why I called out just now. My thinking seems to come and go and I thought I'd better talk to someone while I'm come.'

Lou could hear the smile in his voice and was comforted.

'I'm listening. I've got my note-book too. I can write down anything special.'

'Well, Lou,' said Cop, lying there grey in the shadows and speaking slowly with care, 'the boys know about this short shaft thing already.'

He held it out to her; she could just see it by starlight.

'It came apart and that's why we crashed. But I do all my own maintenance, Lou. If this'd needed attention I know I'd've noticed. I don't want to frighten you but you've got to understand this clearly. *Someone* fiddled that short shaft. It wasn't an accidental accident.'

Lou drew in her breath, but she was determined to be controlled, sensible.

'Do you know who did it or why?' she asked.

'No,' said Cop, 'not who at all. As for why, I suppose it's this secret business I told you about. For some reason it's more important to someone than I'd imagined. It's incredible. I'd no idea. Can't understand. Wish I'd never brought you three along.'

'It's lucky you did,' said Lou bravely, 'or we wouldn't be here to help.'

'Now, Lou. Orders. Listen carefully. Promise to do as I say. I've been lying here, thinking, planning and making decisions. These are your orders and Peter and Ross must understand too.'

'Yes, Cop,' said Lou, wondering what on earth he would 'order' them to do. Not at all like Cop, *orders*.

'First thing,' said Cop, 'if another chopper arrives, you three must run and hide in the bush. Make a plan with Peter and Ross. The person who interfered with the short shaft's almost certain to follow up by looking to see what's happened. Well, he'll find me and perhaps a good thing too. He'll fly me out, I hope. But he meant me to smash, be killed even. I don't think he knows about you kids. Can't believe anyone'd sabotage kids. So I don't *want* him to know about you, don't want you involved. Shift your gear. Hide. He's dangerous. He mustn't find you. Understand? You've got to disappear.'

'Yes,' gasped Lou.

'Second thing,' went on Cop, though his voice sounded fainter, 'I left the usual emergency routine with Nick, the ranger. You know Nick at Te Anau?'

'Yes,' said Lou again.

'Routine as follows. If I'm overdue fetching your parents from Te Anau, he'll pop over to Dolphin Sound. If no one's there he'll go to our bush rendezvous. It's a place where a chopper can land. In a valley. Near a creek. About half-way between the cottage and Te Anau. Lou, this is the very secret thing. This place, this rendezvous place, it's the place I wanted to explore. The secret place. Even Nick doesn't know that. Don't tell him. Don't tell anybody. You three must get to this place and eventually Nick'll find you. Then tell Nick where I am. I suppose I may see Nick first if – if this other joker flies me out. You know Nick, the ranger, Nick, don't you?'

'Yes Cop, yes, yes,' Lou repeated, 'I told you. We know Nick.' She was terrified Cop would slip into unconsciousness before he had explained where this special place was.

'Pencil and paper,' said Cop, his voice slurring.

Lou fumbled with the button of her pocket, pulled out her note-book and pencil. She put the pencil in Cop's right hand, held the note-book steady for him. He began to draw, talking as he did so.

'Think it'd be downstream from here, south-ish.' He

sketched a rough compass. 'Not sure. On clear day, climb above bush, look down. Look for lake. This shape. Island off a peninsula. Looks like a finger pointing at this island.' Cop drew a wobbly shape, then pencilled in a line from the tip of the peninsula, through the island, on across the lake and then on again.

'This place you've to go to, see, it's about four times as

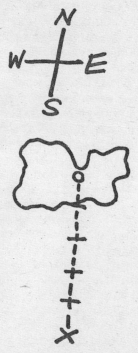

far as the width of the lake, in straight line, from here ...' His words petered out but he went on with his line till it measured four times the width of the lake. There he put a big X.

'That's the spot. X marks the spot.'

'I understand,' said Lou. 'We've to find X. Nick'll meet us there. We mustn't tell anyone it's the secret place.'

'Good girl,' whispered Cop.

'Oh, but Cop!' cried Lou, suddenly realizing the full implications of what she had said, 'one of us must stay with you. We can't leave you alone and hurt.'

Cop could scarcely speak. 'Lou,' he gasped. *'Orders. I'm okay ... with food, water. You three stick together. Find X. Must find X. Nick ...'*

He was drifting, mumbling. His head rolled sideways and Lou stuffed the blanket back under it. She waited a little while, too cold even to shiver. Cop seemed to be asleep. She took the torch, climbed down and scurried back to the tent. She put the note-book into her shirt pocket, buttoned down the flap, wriggled back to her sleeping-bag. She was so cold she thought she would never get back to sleep, but the roar of the waterfall seemed to hypnotize her. The next moment, it seemed, it was daylight, and Peter and Ross were talking in low voices.

'I can't understand *why*,' Peter was saying, and Ross was wishing Cop had told them the whole story instead of nattering about possums.

Lou sat up. Peter hoped she had not heard any remarks about the helicopter being tampered with; girls got in such panics. He tried to convey this message to Ross and was so busy nudging him that he only half-heard Lou's opening remarks, which were straight to the point.

'That short shaft,' Lou was saying, 'you realize, do you, someone fiddled it and that's why we crashed?'

'Well!' exploded Peter. 'Is that so? You know all about such things, do you?'

'Yes,' said Lou with dignity. 'Cop woke in the night and told me all about it. And lots of other very important things. Our marching orders, in fact.'

They sat hunched up in their sleeping-bags listening to Lou. At first Peter refused to accept the order to leave Cop, but the more they discussed it, the more they understood the reasons. Three children in the bush together were much safer than two children. And if Cop did not want

26

the man to know of the children's presence, well, what would that child do if the man flew in to inspect Cop? Lou showed them the map Cop had drawn.

'X marks the spot,' she explained, 'and it's an absolute secret. That X is also the area Cop wanted to explore. Even Nick doesn't know that. It's where he'll look for us, though, when he realizes we're overdue.'

'Well, we'd better get moving,' said Ross enthusiastically. 'Don't rescue parties always set out at first light?'

Lou looked across at Peter.

'It's not like that, is it?' she asked. 'It's not Nick who'll be out looking for us.'

'Why on earth?' began Ross, turning to Peter. 'Dad and Mum, they'll put people on to it.'

'Lou's right,' said Peter. 'Dad and Mum don't know we're lost. They think we're at the cottage. It won't be till Cop doesn't fetch them, say in another three weeks, well, *that's* when they'll realize something's wrong.'

Ross saw his mistake, quickly recovered his bounce.

'Ross Crusoe, that's me,' he said cheerfully, 'camping holidays a speciality. Except for these something sandflies.'

He swiped uselessly at the black cloud of insects that hovered and attacked.

'Chuck us some of that Poof stuff, Lou.'

Lou sighed. Ross was so young sometimes.

'Do I have to spell it out?' she said. '*Nick* won't come for three weeks. But the somebody who fiddled that shaft thing'll check up on Cop to see if his plan's worked. I reckon we can expect a visitor quite soon.'

'Exactly,' agreed Peter.

Ross broke in.

'I know what we need,' he shrilled, 'a plan of campaign. This is war.' He hurried on, bursting with ideas. 'Now, say this joker arrives, what do we do? We don't have to hide. We can play it tough. We've even got Cop's rifle, we could force him at gunpoint to fly us out; there's the axe too. We could hi-jack his chopper.'

Lou turned to Peter and said in her superior voice that made Ross furious, 'Watching too much television, I think.'

Peter ignored both Ross and Lou and climbed out of his sleeping-bag, applying Poof as he did so.

'Come on, move. We've got to obey Cop's orders. Collect your own gear, stow it in your packs and hide the lot in the fern. Then we'll divide the food and fix up Cop. If you hear a chopper coming, run.'

'Where'll we run to?' asked Lou. 'Cop said to make a plan.'

'There's that shallow cave by the waterfall,' said Peter, 'as good as anywhere. If we can remove traces of our existence that type'll never even look for us. Now hurry up.'

Peter and Lou and Ross went into action. All three knew what they had to do and, now they were properly awake, realized how urgent it was to clear the camp. Lou went to look at Cop, who was asleep, or unconscious. He looked awful but was breathing regularly. She tried, and failed, to take his pulse. She had never taken anyone's pulse before. Not that it would have helped, since she did not know the normal pulse rate.

By the time she was back the boys had rolled up the sleeping-bags. Then each of them checked their clothes; a waterproof parka, spare jersey and socks. Peter and Ross wore tramping boots; Lou was less well off with canvas basketball boots. Everyone wore jeans and bush shirts. Everyone had a pocket knife and whistle. As they shoved things into their packs, each added a few extras. Peter grabbed a plastic bag to keep his matches dry and, with memories of trying to light a fire with damp kindling, he added a candle. Ross took his torch, for signalling – 'I nearly know Morse,' he explained to Lou, 'it's just a matter of choosing easy words.' He also had a compass. Lou thought of the first-aid kit in the chopper and stuffed some sweets into her pocket, along with pencils and the sketch book with Cop's map. Peter was to take the ammunition and rifle, Ross the nylon rope, and Lou put the tent, in its canvas cover, with her belongings.

'Now food,' said Peter, looking round with approval. Things were going well.

'What say we light a fire before we go?' suggested Ross. 'At a safe distance,' he added hurriedly. 'Then before we set off, put on some damp stuff and make plenty of smoke. To guide in our friend the villain and with luck he'll take Cop to hospital right away. I don't fancy Cop in that cockpit, all alone, for three weeks.'

'Nor do I,' agreed Peter, 'but smoke mightn't show above the mountain mist. I suppose we could try.' He spoke doubtfully, something nagging at the back of his mind.

'We've still not decided about the food,' said Lou. 'How much to take and how much to leave with Cop. I think Cap ought to have most because he can't help himself, but we can pick berries and, er ... catch fish.'

'On the other hand,' said Ross, 'not meaning to sound greedy, but he'll be lying still. We've got to chop through that bush. Talk about dense. Look at it! And we've got to get above the bush line on to the tops to hunt for that lake.'

They both turned to Peter.

'Better leave most with him,' Peter decided. 'We'll take the rifle. We're sure to find deer. We'll be right. You fix it, Lou. I think Ross and I'll chop wood for that fire.'

So to Lou's consternation the ration decision was left to her. It turned out not to be so very difficult because they had very little food with them anyway, just the emergency supplies in the helicopter and a few last-minute extras. (Cop had flown most of the provisions in to the cottage the week before, along with the fuel.) She left Cop most of the tins and a tin opener, and filled the two big billies with water for him. She put some Poof and aspirin handy. For themselves she took a plastic bag of oatmeal, three tins of stew and beans, some meat cubes, lemon crystals and glucose sweets. She put four boxes of matches in each pack and a tube of Poof.

Peter and Ross were starting away at a dead tree a hundred yards down the valley. Lou could have done with their help, dragging the packs and equipment into the fern.

At last it was done. Lou went back to the cockpit. Unconscious, Cop's face was smooth, the creases of pain relaxed. He looked peaceful. He still held the short shaft.

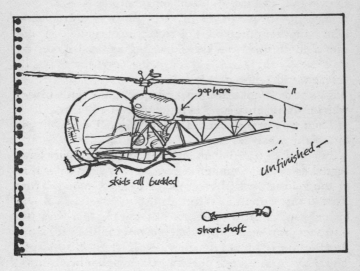

What next? Lou went and flopped down in the shade, worn out. She took out her note-book and pencil and, just for the record, began to sketch the wrecked helicopter.

'It could be used in evidence,' she thought, drawing an arrow to indicate the gap where the short shaft had broken away. Lou had watched a good many television thrillers too.

Out of the corner of her eye she saw Peter and Ross suddenly stop their work and stare upwards. Lou had been conscious of how loudly the waterfall was roaring; she now realized that the increased noise was not the waterfall at all. The next moment a helicopter skimmed over the crags above them. Lou hurled herself under the cover of the trees as the craft hovered for a few moments, circled over their little valley and then began to descend.

It seemed the cliff face would split with the noise of the helicopter; tussock, leaves and dirt whirled up in a frenzied haka dance of challenge. Lou struggled and ripped her way through the bush towards the waterfall. Not far behind, Peter and Ross came charging along. They overtook Lou, led the way into the hollow in the cliff face. The spray from the waterfall blew back into the cave and drenched them. They were well hidden in shadow, yet could see into the valley through the tangled curtains of creepers and hanging moss.

The helicopter landed, the engine cut, the rotor blades whirled on in silence. Perhaps it was Nick?

Then two transparent doors opened. Two men got out. Neither was Nick.

Suddenly Peter remembered why he should never have agreed to cutting wood for a fire. The realization hit him in the stomach and then crept icily up his spine. Trust Ross to think up an idea like that. But Peter knew it was his responsibility: and he had left Lou to deal with the stores and stack up an obvious pile of provisions for Cop. *And* he himself had left the short shaft in the cockpit. These men would see at once that Cop had not been alone. Two men. Two men would search.

Ross was making suggestions.

'Sure they aren't Nick's friends? Sure it wouldn't be better to put in an appearance? They don't look like crooks.'

His brother and sister jabbed him fiercely.

'Shut up and watch.'

'They can't hear,' objected Ross, 'not with this waterfall ...' His sentence trailed off. Peter and Lou simply

31

were not listening, both were concentrating on the scene that was now taking place, in pantomime, on the open-air stage of the valley.

Peter was scrutinizing the helicopter that had just arrived. It appeared to be the same make as Cop's. Identical, yes, but without dual control. Same fuel system, 17-gallon tank each side. Lou was fixing the appearance of the two characters into her mind's eye.

'I'll draw them later,' she thought. 'Just by watching how they behave we'll know if they're friends or not. I must remember every detail.'

It even occurred to Ross, at this point, that he might be required to pick out photographs, or better still, take part in one of those identity parades. All you had to do was touch the person you recognized.

The two men walked away from the whirling circumference of the rotor arm. Neither seemed in any hurry. Apart from sharing this casual attitude, which proved they could not care less whether Cop were dead or alive, the two men could hardly have been less alike.

Lou was fascinated by the tall man. She did not really approve of his appearance, but he epitomized every idolized male whose photographs she had seen in glossy overseas magazines. Perhaps he was this year's top Oscar award winner; or a champion racing driver; the greatest ever bullfighter; the sportsman of the year; the new dictator of some South American state. His clothes were fabulous. A snow-white high-necked pullover and light brown slacks. Were they made of leather? They clung to his slim hips like a second skin and the bottoms were tucked casually into squashy-looking fringed leather boots.

As Lou's imagination came down to earth and she examined him more carefully she was disappointed to realize he was older than she had first imagined. His head was going bald and his sideburns were too showy. His black hair curled over his collar, as though it had slipped back off the slippery dome of his skull. On reflection Lou decided that this 'maturity' enhanced, if anything, the aura of money and power and glamour that had struck her so forcibly as a first impression.

Peter summed up this man in two words, 'the Boss'. He was much more interested in the second man, an ordinary down-to-earth individual in bush shirt and jeans and tramping boots. He was stockier and younger than the other man, less brain, more brawn; his shoulders were broad, his neck short and thick.

'That's the one we'd have to deal with,' thought Peter. 'He's a bushman, that one. Wonder how he got mixed up with that play-boy type.'

At that moment a flock of long-tailed birds swept over the clearing and into the trees on the far side, screeching and chattering. In an instant the Boss had a huge pair of binoculars to his eyes. Peter stared at the super-binoculars, Lou watched the birds ('Parakeets I think') and it was only Ross who was still watching the other man. The moment the Boss's attention had been diverted, this other fellow pulled a curved bottle of something out of a capacious pocket, unscrewed the lid and had four or five huge gulps, before slipping the bottle unobtrusively away. The Boss did not notice. Or if he did, he made no sign of having noticed.

'Ooo! he's a boozer,' leered Ross cheerfully, 'that little one. He drinks. That's *his* hang-up.'

By now the Boss was peering into the smashed helicopter, leaning over Cop. He beckoned Boozer to have a look. Then the Boss relaxed nonchalantly on the tussock where the tent had been pitched. He was no fool. His hand was ruffling up the flattened grass and he showed no surprise when Boozer passed something down to him. It was the short shaft.

Boozer now climbed up to inspect the gap where the short shaft should have been. The Boss rose to his feet and, using the short shaft as a conductor's baton, pointed out first Cop's pile of stores, secondly the trampled tussock, and thirdly the half-chopped branches where Peter and Ross had been working. He was giving instructions.

Then, elegantly, in those beautiful boots, the Boss sauntered towards the fringe of the forest.

Lou gasped. He was almost on top of the packs she had hidden in the fern. But the hiding-place was in deep shadow and the morning sun dazzled the man. He took a few steps to the side, under the trees and then, systematically, with those enormously powerful binoculars, he started to scan the surrounding bush. He was poised effortlessly, turning inch by inch; slowly, slowly those two huge black eyes swung towards the children. Now he was facing the cave.

'Don't move,' muttered Peter, 'freeze.'

'Turned to ice,' Ross said through clenched teeth, to prove he was not even moving his lips.

The lenses seemed to hesitate. Lou felt the black circles were twin magnets that would draw her out of hiding. She remembered how she had very nearly worn her scarlet shirt when she left home and had changed to the dark green one for no particular reason. Did God arrange things like that? It seemed impossible and yet ... Now the man had swung to examine a different area of bush and the children unfroze.

'What on earth is Boozer up to?' whispered Ross.

In the small doorway of the helicopter Boozer was installed, busy with some small instrument and Cop's stack of food.

'He's got the tin opener,' gasped Lou. 'How mean can you get?'

'They're going to eat the lot,' muttered Peter. 'Greedy brutes.'

It was almost worse than that. Boozer simply emptied out the food and scuffed it about with his boot.

'He's been told to spoil it,' said Peter. 'The Boss hopes that's our entire stock and if we see it go we'll come out and give ourselves up. Too bad.'

'I don't care what they do,' said Lou, 'if only they'll help Cop. They don't seem to care a rap about him. Pete, they won't just go away and leave him, will they?'

Peter was beginning to wonder that too.

By now the Boss was back at the helicopter and it seemed that the problem of Cop was under discussion. Eventually Boozer was sent to the other helicopter for an axe and set to work chopping poles. The Boss took no part in these proceedings but dabbed his chin and hands with insect repellent and put his binoculars back to his eyes.

'He's watching the parakeets and bush canaries,' said Lou. 'He's forgotten about us.'

'Just couldn't care less,' said Peter.

'Oho!' said Ross, 'there's Boozer at the bottle again. *And* he's the pilot. Talk about drink and drive.'

Boozer was working hard as well as indulging. The first poles were used for splinting Cop – not that the children could see, but they could feel that something complicated was going on; eventually the Boss deigned to help, and between them the two men hauled Cop, stiff as a ramrod, out on to the tussock. Boozer now lashed him on to a Scout-style stretcher, made with two more poles and a couple of inside-out parkas.

'How'll they fit all that into their chopper?' asked Lou.

'Gee, I hope one of them doesn't stay behind,' put in Ross. 'I'll simply have to move soon. To spread on more Poof. I'm in agonies.'

'Thank heavens Cop's unconscious,' said Peter, and Ross felt rebuked, knowing Peter was weighing sandfly bites against Cop's injuries.

'Well, how *will* they take him?' Lou persisted.

'On the skids,' said Peter grimly.

'Wow!' exclaimed Ross, forgetting the rebuke. Lou shuddered. It was all very well to lash supplies to the skids, but Cop . . .

It was soon done.

The Boss, still immaculate, climbed into his seat and fastened his safety belt without a second glance at the burden on the skids.

Boozer paused. The Boss handed out binoculars through the open plastic door and this time it was Boozer who scanned the bush. The sun had moved by now and fell brightly on the children. Even Ross had misgivings, realizing that the friendly shadows had gone and only a tangle of bush lay between themselves and those powerful eyes.

The man noticed a rainbow against the cliff, where the spray from the waterfall caught the sun. The children crouched motionless, unaware that they were completely invisible, hidden by a veil of seven colours.

Boozer handed back the binoculars, slammed the door and, running round the nose, boarded the helicopter from the other side. Within a few seconds the engine roared to life, the wind from the rotor blades whipped up the dust, and then the noise increased tenfold as the engines revved and the helicopter rose in the air. The children watched it go, with Cop on the skids, like a man performing a terrifying circus act. Then the sound waves broke over the edges of the valley and the noise dispersed. The helicopter soared away out of sight.

CHAPTER THREE

Ross was about to dash out, but Peter held him back. 'They may be circling round, trying to spot us from the air up on the tops,' he said.

Ross scowled. It was no use. Lou would only side with Peter if he started to argue.

So they waited. Shivered and waited, drenched in spray and longing to get into action.

'We'll make straight for the bush and follow the creek down and put a few miles between us and here,' said Peter.

'Didn't Cop say we were to go up on the tops and have a look-see?' objected Ross.

'Well, we will, but not here and not yet,' snapped Peter. 'Those two might take Cop to Te Anau and come straight back to do a thorough search for us. We mustn't be around.'

'Supposing,' said Lou, 'just supposing Cop tells them at the hospital where we are and sends Nick for us. Oughtn't we to be here?'

'And suppose Cop doesn't, suppose he's still unconscious or . . .' Peter did not want to say "dead" . . . 'Or they don't take him to hospital . . . or something. No, our orders were absolutely clear. Find X. X marks the spot. All we've got to do is to get ourselves to X and stay alive for three weeks and then we can be certain Nick'll find us.'

'That's certainly what Cop said,' agreed Lou; and Ross, outnumbered, shrugged his shoulders and shut his mouth.

After about ten minutes they judged it safe to come out from cover. They rescued the packs from the fern and helped each other hump them on to their backs. Peter looked at the lop-sided loads.

'We'll go for an hour or so,' he said, 'and then stop and reorganize ourselves. Cop always says a well-balanced pack is half the battle. No time now, though. Let's off.'

With a last brief glance at the smashed helicopter and

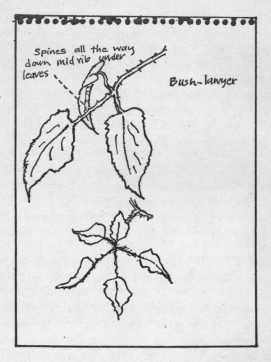

Spines all the way down midrib under leaves

Bush-lawyer

the swarm of insects devouring the spoilt food, he slung his rifle over one shoulder, grabbed the axe and led the way to the creek. Lou had tied the tent to her pack and Ross had coiled the rope round his in one giant tangle of knots. They lurched after Peter, almost running, and followed him along the gravel beach, but after three hundred yards or so the creek disappeared into a tunnel of deep bush.

Peter halted for a moment, summing up the situation. On each side of the creek the banks now rose steeply; trees hung down right over the water which was rushing down this narrow gully fast and yellow and deep. Peter brandished the axe and began to slash aside the creepers that festooned the lolling branches. Ross and Lou pushed through after him. It was thrilling to plunge into that dark tangle. All the pretend games of heroism and endurance which they had played in the bush near home had now become a serious reality. Even Lou, who was a little bit afraid, felt exhilarated; having to overcome her fear was tremendously exciting.

They would have stumbled less if they had carried no loads. The awkward weight on their backs upset their sense of balance and the straggling bush-lawyer clung to their packs with its sharp hooks, snagged the straps, caught at the rifle and the rope and ripped at their faces and arms. They put down their heads and charged forwards, followed by a deliriously dancing cloud of sandflies, which settled in thick black swarms on any area where Poof had not been thickly spread. One trouble was that the children got so hot, the sweat washed away the Poof and the sandflies moved in immediately to the attack. Lou resolved to ignore sandflies completely, just let them crawl and bite; she had heard of the triumph of mind over matter and this was just the moment to put the philosophy into practice. Actually she was finding the going harder than the boys were, being taller and more leggy, less athletic.

After half an hour it was Peter who called a halt.

'Pause for rest,' he gasped, swiping at sandflies. 'Don't know how far we've gone. Not more than about half a mile, I'm afraid. It's mighty tough out here in front. Anyone else like a turn?'

'But the Boss and Boozer won't find us now,' said Lou. She ignored Peter's question; she did not want to lead at all.

They all smeared themselves again with Poof.

'Just getting a drink,' said Ross. Slipping off his pack, he scrambled to the creek. It was hard to get right down to water level; the fallen trees made a latticework above the creek. Suddenly a rotten branch broke and immediately Ross *was* down at water level, in fact below it. The current caught him as he splashed, and before he could grab at anything or find the breath to shout he was swept away downstream.

Lou was stunned with horror. Peter leapt into action: dropped the rifle, wriggled madly out of his pack and crashed off downstream after Ross. Within thirty seconds the first danger was over. Ross had grabbed at a boulder which had halted him long enough for him to sight and snatch at a branch above his head. He was clinging to it now with both hands, his feet were against another boulder and he was bracing himself against the current. The water foamed up round his legs, like gaiters of froth.

Peter thrashed his way to the edge of the creek, wishing he had brought the rope. He scrambled out along a fallen tree; Ross had hold of one of its lowest branches.

'I'm here, hang on!' he bellowed, but he was three feet above Ross's head. How he needed that rope; if only Lou would have the sense to bring it.

Poor Lou, she did have the sense, but there she was down on her knees, trying, trying to undo the knots with which Ross had lashed the coil of rope to his pack. Ross did such tough knots. Lou broke her nails, yanked with her teeth.

Ross gasped, 'Can't hold on for ever.'

Peter wedged one foot under the branch, curled the other leg round it, whipped off his jersey and wrapped the end of one sleeve round his right hand.

'Grab this and heave up!' he shouted, dangling the jersey over his brother's head and clinging with all his might to the branch with his left arm.

Ross wasted no time. He knew he must make the effort

while he had the strength to do so. He managed to haul on his branch, straighten his knees against the rock and grab the jersey with one hand, then with both. His feet slipped and his legs were swept away from under him. The jersey stretched but did not rip. Peter hauled, Ross bent his elbows in an almighty chin-up. The next moment he was clear of the water's pull and Peter had him by one wrist. Ross got his legs up into a monkey crawl along the branch and then with another heave he was astride it. Peter had him by the collar now. Ross rested for a moment, gathering his strength again. Then the brothers slowly wriggled back along the branch to the bank.

Lou was still angry with the rope and suddenly was furious with Ross for giving her such a fright, taking such risks, soaking his clothes and especially for tying up the rope so tightly.

'What a daft, crazy thing to do,' she cried. 'Tie up a rope so no one can undo it, nearly pull Peter in on top of you –'

Peter interrupted her, remembering his mother had the same curious habit of being angry to cover up fear.

'But he's safe and so am I, so cheer up, Lou. Anything to eat to help us recover?'

Ross was lying face down on the moss trying to wake himself up from the nightmare of nearly being drowned. But when Lou, who was already ashamed of her outburst, took six sweets from her pocket, he sat up again and grinned at her. He was a very resilient boy.

'Ice-cold water's marvellous for sandfly bites,' he assured her, 'very soothing. You must try it some time.'

Peter began to put on his jersey again. One sleeve was now stretched six inches longer than the other. He was sweating hot, but the jersey helped to keep sandflies at bay.

As Lou gave them two sweets each, she said diffidently, 'We might as well repack now and tie on the rope, well, differently. Ross, you'd better get dry.'

41

'I'm not taking off a single stitch,' said Ross. 'The sand-flies are queuing up for me to undress and I'm jolly well going to disappoint them. I'll soon dry off on the move.'

'Yes,' agreed Peter, 'I'm for going a bit further before repacking. I keep hearing that chopper.'

So they set off again. Ross took a turn in front, wielding the axe and warming up till his clothes steamed. Lou bit back governessy remarks about deaths of cold, pneumonia; Ross never came to any harm, though he took more risks than any other person Lou knew. She stumbled along behind her brothers and hoped his luck would continue to hold.

The bank close to the creek became literally impenetrable. Gradually they were forced away from the creek and after a while found a faint deer track, not a path, just a way through that was less dense than elsewhere. Here and there, where a fallen tree trunk had to be climbed, there was a gash in the bark, showing rust-red against the moss which had been scuffed aside by a hoof. On their right the creek was roaring – in fact, as Peter had said, roaring noises came from everywhere; some could have been the helicopter, or else the wind in the tall trees. The children could not see up through the leaf ceiling to the sky and knew at least that no one in the sky could see them down in the gloom under the trees. It was like a cave, deep down under the sea, and the looping vines were seaweed and the fungi grew like barnacles over the smashed-up wrecks of broken trees.

Peter followed Ross, thankful to be free of the responsibility of leading. Lou came last, her eyes fixed on Peter's legs, thrusting on and on, up and down, like pistons. It was all she could do to keep up. She concentrated on putting her feet exactly where his had trodden, with the tune of *Good King Wenceslaus Looked Out* jigging endlessly through her head in time with her steps.

After another half hour Ross stopped and stood listening. Peter had been dimly conscious for the last ten minutes that something was peculiar about the creek, but now he could hear what it was. The roar of water no longer came from their right. It seemed to be on their left. Or was it? Lou was listening too. She moved her head from side to side, like a dog trying to pick up a scent. Ross was stumped for a few moments. Then he remembered his compass and fished it out of his still-damp back pocket.

'I'd forgotten about this,' he said cheerfully. 'It'll soon get us right. Let's think. We're meant to be travelling about south-south-west, I suppose.'

He turned the compass round till north lay under the needle. Peter and Lou watched.

'Well, that's not bad,' he said. 'I'm facing almost due south at the moment.'

'Well, how come the creek has changed sides?' asked Lou. 'We didn't cross it anywhere.'

'I wonder if somehow we've gone in a circle,' said Peter, 'it can happen in the bush. And we haven't actually seen the creek for nearly half an hour.'

'Now I come to think of it,' said Lou, 'I know this sounds ridiculous . . . but are you sure we're facing the way we're going?'

The boys looked at her pityingly. Lou tried again.

'I mean,' she said unhappily, looking all around, 'for the last few minutes we've been turning this way and that, looking at the compass and so on. Where exactly did we come from? I don't think we're facing straight ahead any more. I somehow thought we passed *that* log just before Ross stopped.'

'Oh, heavens no,' cried Ross, 'we came from over there' – he pointed at right angles to the log – 'didn't we, Peter?'

Peter bent down to look closely at the undergrowth.

'Haven't the faintest idea,' he admitted. 'Of course an Aborigine or a Red Indian'd spot a cracked twig and a bent blade of grass straight away. But I'm dashed if I can see any tracks anywhere.'

They were all silent for a few moments. The creek

43

seemed to roar from every direction. On all sides trees towered, moss hung in festoons, leaves dripped. A school-boy compass was useless in primeval forest.

Peter was suddenly aware of the awful threat of the bush, of his own insignificance and incompetence against its dominating power. He tried to shake off this feeling.

'Bush can't think,' he said, half-aloud, '*I* can think. *I* can win,' and he cast his mind back to recall exactly when it was the creek changed sides.

Lou was remembering how, when she was three, she had lost sight of her mother at the Industries Fair, and now she re-lived the terror that had gripped her, hemmed in by people and people, all the same, in every direction. It was like that here, with trees instead of people. 'But I'm big now,' she told herself, 'I can think out what to do.'

Out loud she said, 'Brainwork needed.' She picked up a stick and choosing a green slimy rock as a blackboard she began to sketch a map which showed up white like chalk.

'Here's the creek,' she explained as she drew. 'At first it went south-west. Here's us, following it, then turning farther south away from the creek after Ross fell in. Now we can hear water on our left, so ...' She held the stick poised, thinking hard. Then she continued the line of the creek with a swoop eastwards.

'That's it!' exclaimed Peter. 'You've got it, Lou. The creek must do a big bend. There's no reason for it to flow steadily eastwards, it could even double back north, or in any direction. By heading for it by ear we'll pick it up further downstream and save ourselves a long walk round all the wiggles. It'll be flowing from our right to our left when we reach it,' and he added two arrows to Lou's map to show the direction of the current.

'That's splendid, then,' cried Ross. 'Of course I led you this-a-way on purpose, because I realized it'd be a short cut.'

He joked because he was so tremendously relieved. It had been humiliating to feel they had got lost while he was leader.

Peter shouldered his pack once more and slung the rifle round his neck for a change.

'How about you leading for a bit, Lou?' he suggested. 'Straight for the creek and then we'll stop to eat.'

'All right,' said Lou, much cheered by having solved the problem before the boys. She set off at a slower pace than Ross had done, remembering that a steady speed is less tiring than an erratic one.

It was not difficult now to head for the noise of the creek. It sounded quite near and louder all the time, yet it was further away than seemed possible. Lou's legs were so tired they would hardly do as she told them. She stumbled on and on; where had the wretched creek got to? Could they possibly be wrong again? The drumming roar of the water seemed so close it could have been inside her head; over every rise she expected to see the creek thundering down its gully, but it was never there. She glanced over her shoulder at the boys and recognized the look on their faces. They were now feeling as she had felt until she was leader, so tired that they were remote from their surroundings, relying simply on following in the footsteps of the person ahead.

'I'll find that creek or drop,' Lou told herself, scrambling over a giant fallen tree, squelching down into a bog of spongy moss on the other side. Her boots were sodden through, her clothes steamed with damp and heat. She pushed between the ferns, tripped over the crumbling dead fronds. Then she stopped. Ross did not notice in time and crashed into her. Further back, Peter slithered to a standstill in the bog.

In a deep gully below rushed the creek at last. It was whipped up into yellow foam as it hurtled over the boulders and fallen trees. The deafening roar that they had been hearing for so long was not the sound of the creek itself but of a huge waterfall that leapt a hundred feet or more into the chasm below them.

Peter and Ross climbed up beside Lou. None of them said a word. It was obvious at once that they had been wrong in their calculations. Peter had drawn in his arrow on Lou's plan to show the water running from west to east, from their right to their left as they faced the creek. And here was a creek running in completely the opposite direction, from east to west. Up on the left was the waterfall and the water foamed and swirled past them towards the right. This could not possibly be their creek at all. So now what?

CHAPTER FOUR

THEY sat down in silence. The sandflies became ecstatic and swarmed over them. The children rubbed on more Poof and Peter looked at his watch.

'It's after six,' he said.

'We never really had any lunch, let alone breakfast,' said Ross.

'I wonder where Cop is now?' said Lou.

'Camp here?' suggested Peter, and there was no need to ask the question. None of them could have gone any further. The problem of the creek was too great to be considered on an empty stomach.

'A decent meal and a night's sleep,' Lou said, trying, and failing, to sound cheerful, wondering how to muster enough energy for the tasks that still lay ahead.

Peter struggled to his feet.

'Come on,' he encouraged them, 'a big hot fire and food and then to sleep in the warmth and wake up in the morning feeling a box of birds.'

He began to drag some stones together to make a fire-place. Ross crawled to his feet and started ripping the papery bark off a fuchsia tree, to use for kindling. Lou took the tent out of her pack. There did not seem to be anywhere remotely flat or clear on which to pitch it. Then Peter dragged a branch over to the fire-place and, seizing the axe, cleared away some undergrowth, leaving a reasonable tent site.

'You help Lou, Ross,' he said, 'I'll do the fire.'

He took out his candle, cut off an inch of it, fixed it between two stones in his fire-place. He lit the wick and piled shreds of fuchsia bark round it; but they were too damp. They put out the candle – All around was wood, but it was saturated, soggy, squelchy. Peter resolved that in future he would always dry some kindling for the next fire. 'So I'll only have to do it this once,' he told himself, and began to chop into a huge log. He knew the heart of it would be dry enough to start a fire; the very heart. He chopped and chopped and his arms felt as weak as a scarecrow's. But he had to go on, so he did.

Lou and Ross were faring rather better with the tent, not that the spongy moss looked very warm to sleep on. Ross ripped off dead tree-fern fronds and stuffed armfuls of them into the tent. The sleeping-bags were chucked on top. It looked cosy but the fern fronds were wet like everything else.

By now Peter had enough heart wood to light his fire. He balanced slivers of it in a little triangle over the vacillating candle flame and placed chips round this pyramid, and soon the fire began to take hold. All three children were dragging branches for fuel and building up the blaze. This was a lesson they had learnt when camping with their father: to make an enormous fire and cook, not over flame heat, but over red-hot embers.

As soon as the sun began to sink, darkness fell quickly in the bush. The sandflies, crazy for light, committed suicide by thousands in the fire; hundreds plunged into the billy of stew and beans that Lou was stirring. She could do nothing to stop that. She was past caring anyway.

'It's all good protein,' she told Ross, who was not quite past caring.

'Yes,' he said. '*Our* blood. Attractive.'

'Lovely gravy,' said Lou, surprised to find she could even attempt to joke.

When the moment came to eat, Ross forgot to be squeamish and wolfed down the food. They had boiled some stagnant water from a pool for nearly a quarter of an hour, which they hoped would kill off most of the doubt-less vile organisms it contained; now Lou dissolved lemon crystals in it and they drank it down good and hot.

'Very nourishing,' Lou said, which was the sort of cliché the boys usually pounced on. But they had no energy for arguing and it certainly was a delicious brew.

They built up the fire to a real inferno. The damp logs sizzled, steamed and caught fire. The children dried their clothes as well as they could, and also a pile of kindling. Peter took some of this into the tent and stuffed it down his sleeping bag to make sure it stayed dry. He was not go-ing to cut out heart wood again if he could help it. Peter could feel rain coming.

It was bitterly cold next morning and, sure enough, pouring with rain. When Lou woke she sat up and her head touched the tent. At once the canvas leaked and water trickled down her neck.

'Yow!' squeaked Lou, and woke up the others. 'It's not waterproof,' she protested, 'it's raining down my neck.'

Ross chuckled. Peter said in a sleepy growl, 'Remind me to give you a lecture on surface tension one of these days.'

The tent was throbbing with rain; every now and then water that had been held up by the leaves in the tree tops escaped with a rush and cascaded down, rattling on the canvas. The background roar of the waterfall and the creek sounded like trains in an underground tunnel. When the boys sat up, cautiously, there were sucking, squelchy noises beneath them, as bubbles escaped from the spongy moss.

Peter looked from Lou's white face to Ross's purplish one. They appeared to be even colder than he was him-self, which was icy. But at least all three had had a good sleep and now the day's adventures were waiting.

'Have to keep on the move today,' said Peter cheerfully, 'too cold to hang around. And we might as well make up our minds to it, we're going to get soaked to the skin.'

'I suppose the fire's out,' said Lou gloomily.

'I'll go and look,' said Peter, determined to keep up morale. He began wriggling about, trying to find his parka which was somewhere at the bottom of his pack.

Ross had an idea.

'You know what? You'd keep drier if you took *off* some of your clothes, Pete.'

'Ha-ha,' said Peter, unable to see the joke, but presuming such an idiotic remark was supposed to be funny.

'No, I mean it,' insisted Ross. 'Once you soak those jeans they'll never dry out on a day like this. But wet bare legs soon rub dry.'

The thought of removing anything even remotely warm made Peter come out in goose pimples. But Ross certainly had a point there. Peter remembered he was wearing swimming trunks instead of underpants, and that was certainly an appropriate garment. He pulled off his jeans, put on his boots and then his parka. He had trouble untying the tapes that held the tent flap shut; his fingers were numb and the knots had pulled tight in the wet. Eventually he succeeded and crawled out into the rain. Exactly what happened next, nobody knew. Somehow Peter and a taut guy-rope became entangled; the rope, shrunk by the rain, was probably already straining against the peg that barely held it. The next moment there were 'pings' in all directions, the tent collapsed on Lou and Ross, water flooded everywhere and Peter's theories on surface tension were proved beyond dispute.

Peter pulled his face out of the bog where he had landed and forgot his discomfort in the delight of watching the tent. It heaved and shook; it was very irate and crumpled; it squeaked and emitted some rather strong language. Dark stains of wet, outlining sub-human shapes, mottled the greenish canvas. A pair of feet (Lou's) emerged from one end, and a head (Ross's) shot out of the other. The effect was of a prehistoric tortoise with a squashy shell. While he was laughing at that, Peter discovered that last night's fire was still glowing, and that stopped him laughing because the discovery was made by his putting one hand in the hot ashes. He was not burnt badly, though he yelped when it happened.

When the others had emerged from chaos and struggled into their parkas, Peter announced he was going down to have a look at the creek and to fill the billy with some decent fresh water. With a sideways look at Ross, Lou rather ostentatiously put the rope handy for a quick rescue. Peter thanked her with mock politeness, adding, 'No cold bath this morning; I've already had an exhilarating shower.'

'Well, you do surprise me,' replied Lou. 'No one would've guessed it to look at you.'

The three surveyed each other critically for a moment. Then they all began to laugh again. The situation was ludicrous, too serious to be taken seriously. There was Peter, his face caked with the black mud he had tripped into, though white streaks had appeared where the rain had run off his hair in rivulets. His parka was too small for him and ended high up his thighs, where there was not even a glimpse of his swimming things, so that it appeared that he was naked underneath the parka. Ross still wore his jeans, which were soaked. He looked particularly uncouth because his thick hair had bunched up in front like a peaked cap pulled well down over the eyes. Lou's parka was too big for her; borrowed from her father for the holiday, it came down below her knees and the sleeves reached to the same level, giving her a gorilla effect. She had lost her hair-grip and had trouble in seeing through the dripping curtain of hair hanging over her nose. She tried to sweep it aside with the dangling sleeve to keep it out of her mouth as she laughed at the boys.

'Oh go and get the water then,' she gasped, 'or shall I

just hold out the billy and catch rain? Come on, Ross, I think we'd better get the tent up again somehow so that we can pack under cover. Not quite everything is as soaked as we are.'

'Soon will be,' grunted Ross, prophetically.

This time they packed systematically, dividing the food equally again, putting the spare jerseys to pad the load against their backs. The sleeping-bags were so wet there was nothing much they could do except roll them into the plastic covers and put them at the top of the packs. The outside pockets held the things they were most likely to need during the day: Poof and sweets and sticking-plaster and Peter's dry kindling. While Lou and Ross were pack-ing, Peter had managed to heat up a billy in a pit of ashes. They had a hot drink each, then stirred some rolled oats into the rest of the water and made a mash that was cer-tainly not porridge but was reasonably edible and filling. As they ate, Peter told them about the creek.

'It's three times the depth it was yesterday,' he said. 'You can hardly see any boulders now. I don't think we could possibly cross, even with the rope.'

'Well, we don't want to, do we?' asked Lou.

'I do, I bet I could cross; I'm sure I could,' cried Ross. 'Then I'd tie the rope to the other side for you two . . .'

'I don't mean not want to because it's dangerous,' Lou tried to explain, 'I mean there's no reason to. It's not "our" creek, at least I don't see how it could be, but all creeks go downhill, so this one'll do as well as any other. It'll lead us out to a lake somewhere.'

Peter was doubtful about this.

'You could be right,' he said, 'but I've been trying to draw a map same as you did yesterday, Lou. It seems to me this creek won't lead to a lake, but it's a sort of tribu-tary and it'll join our old creek somewhere down-stream.'

He scratched in the wet ashes and jabbed where his two creeks met.

'We'll land up here, on the tip of this triangle. We'll have to cross one of the creeks eventually.'

'Oh, I see,' said Lou.

'Well, I could do it,' began Ross again.

'You'll probably have to,' Peter snubbed him, 'so save your breath. We'll go downstream and see if I'm right and then decide which creek to cross. One could be easier than the other.'

Ross was getting fed up with having to do what Peter said and Peter always being right. He shrugged his shoulders and said nothing. Misunderstood as usual. He only wanted to help.

Peter rose to his feet and buckled the billy and his mug to the straps of his pack.

'I'll carry the rifle,' he said. 'Lucky I had the ammunition well wrapped in waterproof. Have you both got your matches dry?'

'Mine are in my parka pocket,' said Lou. 'With my knife and whistle and hanky. In a plastic bag.'

'Mine are in the middle of my pack,' said Ross, 'with all my other treasures.'

'Well, I've got ammunition in my parka pocket,' said Peter, 'in case we meet a deer that'd make easy venison. So perhaps my matches'd better go in the pack. They don't mix with gunpowder.'

They cleared the camp, lashed the tent to Lou's pack again and the rope to Ross's. The tent was so heavy with water Lou could hardly lift her pack, but it was not so bad once Peter had heaved it into position, and certainly the careful packing made it more comfortable than on the day before. Peter actually carried less weight than Lou, but the rifle was extremely awkward and while he was leading he had the axe as well.

'No need to fuss about putting out the fire,' said Ross, but he trampled on the charred sticks and scuffed earth over the ashes from force of habit.

'Right! All set? Off we go!' said Peter, and they thrust

their heads forward and braced themselves for another long day.

The bush here was not as dense as the part they had come through the previous day. The trees grew further apart so that on a fine day some sunlight would have reached the forest floor. This meant there were young trees underfoot and moss, with less rot and confusion. They walked along the ridge above the gully. It was pouring with rain, but at least the sandflies seemed to be sheltering from it somewhere; just *not* being bitten was a pleasure in itself. All three of them felt optimistic. Peter, in the lead, felt gloriously fit. He found he could relax as he walked without its affecting his speed. He reckoned fifty miles on a flat road would be child's play after this baptism of fire – or rather, water. He wondered if he could get on one of the Outward Bound courses. Just his line.

Ross, following Peter, had newspaper headlines in his mind's eye. He imagined himself modestly disclaiming heroics but accepting the Queen's Award for bravery – or was that only for policemen? Well, something very grand from the Duke of Edinburgh perhaps, the highest honour for Scouts.

Lou, squelching along at the back, was less egocentric. She was thinking about Cop, hoping they would find their way out before their parents had time to worry about them.

After about three hours they began to hear water on their right as well as from the creek on their left, and shortly afterwards Peter's theory was proved correct. The creek they were following burst out to join another creek, running from the north. Where the waters met, a whirlpool foamed and boiled; then away swept the two creeks together, in an angry torrent, towards the south.

The children stood and watched.

'It makes me feel giddy,' said Lou, after a while. She turned away, heaved off her pack and sat down with her back to both creeks.

54

'Well, we can't cross here,' Peter said. 'Somehow I prefer the look of our Old Friend creek. It looks less boisterous than the Waterfall one. If we explore a bit upstream we might find a reasonable place to cross.'

'Pity we haven't got a canoe,' said Ross. He could see himself, crouching low, manipulating a paddle with incredible skill over the rapids. Lou took out her sketchbook and began damply to sketch a tree fuchsia flower

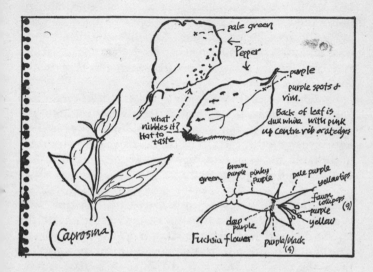

that was dangling in front of her nose. She wanted her next question to sound very casual.

'What's the policy on food?' she asked. 'Something to suck now and open a tin this evening?'

'Suck?' gasped Ross. 'Wow! I'm hungry right now.'

'Pointless remark,' snapped Peter. 'We all are. Saying it makes it worse. We've only got two more tins, so we can't possibly open more than one a day. If only this rain'd stop we might be able to fish or try to shoot something for the pot.'

The other two knew he was right. So they took one beef

cube each. Lou ate hers, crumb by crumb, gloriously salty and strong-tasting. Peter put his in his cheek and let the taste trickle out over his tongue, savouring every drop. Ross wolfed his, swallowing lots of air.

'Makes me feel fuller,' he explained when Lou remonstrated.

'Not if you make noises like that afterwards,' she replied tartly.

They lolled back against tree-stumps and took off their boots and socks and patched up some sore places on their heels and toes. Being sodden through had softened their skin and they all had blisters. Their feet looked white and crinkled, as though they had been too long in the bath.

By this time they had come to terms with the rain and hardly noticed it. It was now at least warm rain, no one was cold – in fact they found it refreshing. After half an hour everyone was keen to be on the move once more and make their first river crossing. They set off up Old Friend Creek to find a suitable place.

About three hundred yards above the junction with Waterfall Creek grew a big old whitey-wood tree. On the far bank a tall lacebark was almost at the water's edge. The children stopped and summed up the possibilities. Even the cautious Lou agreed this place looked reasonable.

'Child's play,' announced Ross.

'Don't you be too sure,' replied Peter. 'Dad's often said that more people are killed in the bush by drowning while crossing rivers than any other way.'

'It's being so cheerful keeps you going,' retorted Ross. 'This place is easy. I'll go over first and tie the rope to that big tree – lacebark or whatever it is.'

Lou was not looking forward to this crossing, but she felt it her duty to protect Ross, who was, after all, the shortest of the three of them, whereas she was the tallest.

'I think I'd better go first, we don't know how deep it is and my legs are longer than yours, Ross.'

She and Ross both turned to Peter for his opinion. At the time he was flattered, but later blamed himself over and over again for perhaps making the wrong decision.

'I don't think it'll matter much about height,' he said.

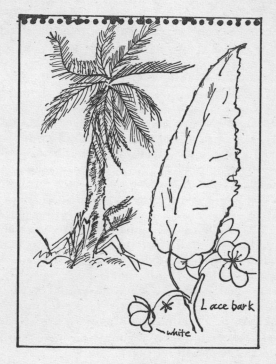

Lace bark

~white

'Ross can go if he wants to. You'll have the rope round you, Ross; Lou and I will pull you in if you stumble. You'll be quite safe.'

'I won't stumble, I'm more sure-footed than Lou,' cried Ross eagerly, while Lou murmured, 'Oh well, if that's what you think,' and was glad to let Ross go.

'Right then,' said Peter, 'come on, packs off.' He untied the rope from Ross's pack and while Lou paid out the loops carefully so that nothing tangled, he tied a firm bowline round the trunk of the whitey-wood. The other end of the rope went round Ross's waist. Peter checked the knot. Then he and Lou took up the slack. Ross received his instructions.

'Aim slightly upstream, Ross; you'll find the current carries you down a bit. When you get across, tie your end of the rope as high as you can reach round the lacebark. Pull in the slack as tight as you can. And mind your bowline.'

'I can tie one with my eyes shut,' protested Ross, getting more and more fed up with Peter's officiousness.

'Well don't, not this time,' advised Lou. Peter ignored both remarks.

'Then Lou'll cross, holding the rope and pushing the packs along. We'll buckle them and they'll hang from the rope. That's why you have to tie it high and pull it tight. Don't want the packs dangling under water.'

'I'm not sure I can manage three packs at once,' said Lou anxiously.

'Oh, I'll be there too,' said Peter loftily. 'When Lou and packs are safe I'll come back again to this side, tie this end of the rope around me and you two haul in the slack as I come across to join you. Okay?'

Ross nodded, Lou was trying to remember what she had heard about crossing rivers.

'Do I cross on the upstream or downstream side of the rope?' she asked. 'I'm sure there's a special reason why one is right and the other isn't.'

'On the upstream side, obviously,' answered Ross at once, 'then there's the rope between you and disappearing downstream.'

'No!' Peter was absolutely emphatic. 'That's how people get drowned. Dad said so. The current swishes them into the rope. They either get all jumbled up in it or their legs float up and they're left hanging by their arms more or less on their backs, all out of control. If you cross below the rope and your legs take off, you can still get across, moving your hands along the rope and half floating on your tummy, like practising your leg-kicking at the deep end of a swimming pool, holding on to the rail.'

Lou tried to imagine herself in each of those situations and did not like either of them, but could see that the second alternative would be easier to manage than the first. She just hoped her legs would stay put on the bottom.

Ross was hacking himself a stout stick with which to test depth; he was also wishing Peter had not been right yet again.

'I'm wet through anyway,' he said, trimming off side shoots with his Scout knife. 'It's not worth taking off my boots.'

'Good heavens no!' cried Peter. 'You need your boots on. They'll help to weigh your feet down. And you can crash along over spikes and jags regardless.'

'That's what I meant,' said Ross quickly.

Now he was ready to start. Peter and Lou took a firm hold of the rope. Ross prodded the water with his stick, then stepped jauntily into the creek. At first the water was fairly shallow, but four feet out there was a sudden shelf. Ross's stick went down two or three feet. Ross followed it boldly. The water was now up to his thighs. He tried to see the bed of the creek, but the water flowed brown as beer, dappled and pock-marked with rain as it hastened to join the other creek at the whirlpool. Ross was astonished to find how difficult it was to walk through such water. He headed upstream as Peter had told him, but realized he was in fact a little further downstream with almost every step. He was glad of that stick as the water got deeper and deeper. And he was even more glad to have his other hand on the rope and feel it taut and safe, jerking slightly as the others paid it out. He almost felt they held him by the hand. Slowly he advanced. It all reminded him a bit too much of yesterday's near escape. He worked his way forwards step by step. Now he was over half-way. He was going to land a good fifteen feet downstream of the lacebark. That did not matter.

Suddenly Ross's foot slid off a hidden rock and for a moment he floundered in the water. But then he was on his knees in the shallows. He had reached the gravel shelf at the far bank. He scrambled out on to the land.

He found he was trembling all over and out of breath. Of course Ross would never admit it, but Peter had been right once more. It was certainly not child's play crossing that current. Ross squared his shoulders, in case the others were watching him, and strode confidently upstream to the lacebark. He had a bit of trouble undoing the knot at his waist; his hands and nails were spongy with wetness. He managed it at last and slung the rope professionally twice round the tree trunk. He hesitated for a moment before tying the bowline. Funny how confusing it was to do a knot round a tree instead of round one's own middle: like tying someone else's tie, sort of back to front. He got the rope good and tight and a decent height above the water. It was lucky the creek was not any wider. There was only about a foot of rope to spare, after the two turns he had given it round the tree. It did not occur to him to tie a safety half-knot in that spare foot. He knew a bowline could not possibly slip.

Ross waved and shouted across to the others, though they could not hear him properly. The creek and the rain and the whirlpool downstream roared in unison. He watched Peter unbuckling the shoulder straps of the three packs and rebuckling them round the rope. He saw Lou edge nervously into the water, her oversized parka bunched up above her waist. She held on to the rope very tightly. Hand over hand she overtook two packs and began pushing the front one which had the axe lashed to it. Now Peter was close behind, shoving and tugging at the other packs. He had taken off his parka and wrapped it round the rifle, which he had fixed, by tying the parka sleeves, like a yoke across his shoulders. They were both managing pretty well. Then Lou stumbled; her legs immediately floated out behind her on the current; she looked ridiculously surprised but held the rope securely, hauling herself up, half out of the water. She had great difficulty trying to get her feet down again; her light canvas boots were no help. However, all was well. Ross clambered down the bank, ready to give her a hand up out of the water. Lou had reached the gravel shelf. Peter looped one arm round the rope; with both hands he managed to untie the rifle and passed it to Lou, who handed it to Ross. Lou turned back again to heave at the nearest pack.

Then the impossible happened. Ross's bowline was suddenly not a bowline after all. The end ran through, the knot disintegrated and there was an almighty splash as three packs and Peter disappeared under the surface. Lou was safe, Ross was hauling her up the gravel. But as he did so he saw Peter swept off in the whirl of the current, away downstream in a trice, over and over he seemed to be tumbling in the water.

Lou screamed. Ross tried to think of everything at once. He grabbed his stick and began running downstream along the bank, hoping somehow he could check Peter by getting ahead of him, holding out the stick for Peter to grab before that nightmare whirlpool. He slithered and stumbled, the rain blew into his eyes. He could not see Peter anywhere.

Then faintly he heard Lou shouting his name and turned for a moment to see her pointing at the far bank. Peter was aground on the gravel over there, still holding the rope. The whitey-wood knot, Peter's bowline, had held firm. Peter had taken off downstream, like a giant fish on a strong line, and had been swept in to the far shore.

Something swelled up and nearly burst inside Ross. He threw out his hands in joy and relief. He waved and shouted to his brother, thumbs up.

Peter too was waving and shouting. He did not look joyful at all. Angrily he was pointing downstream. Ross looked just in time to see one of their packs swallowed up in the whirlpool. Of the other two there was no sign at all.

CHAPTER FIVE

THE next half hour was the worst Ross had ever known. Peter had taken a grip on himself, tied the rope round his waist and again entered the water, as Ross had done originally – only Peter had no guiding hand to pay out the rope or hold him steady. In due course he arrived grim-faced on Lou and Ross's side of the creek. He was so angry that he could hardly speak. Ross's relieved 'At least *you're* safe' approach did nothing to placate him.

'No thanks to you,' spluttered Peter, 'you and your knot! You incompetent little twit, you ...' He suddenly towered over Ross in a frenzy of rage. 'And all our packs have gone. Now we've nothing – no tent, no sleeping-bags, no food; do you understand, *all* our food has gone? Every scrap.' Ross said nothing and Peter stormed on: 'How can we ever get out of here? No food. No shelter. All because you can't be bothered to tie a proper bowline and have to loop up some sort of grannie knot. Did it with your eyes shut, did you, like you said?'

Ross stood in silence, slumped against the tree staring at the river. He did not even seem to be listening. Peter grabbed him roughly, wanting to hurt him.

Lou watched wide-eyed and felt terribly sorry for Ross. Of course he should have taken more care, he always lived from risk to risk. It was the sort of mistake Lou privately felt she might have made too, in the stress of the moment. Ross had been beside himself with joy to see Peter safe, as she had too. Now he was so ashamed he could not even argue, did not even put up an arm to protect himself.

Lou shoved herself between the boys. After all, she *was* the eldest. Fights and hurts would make things worse. She turned to Peter.

'Please shut up, just stop it, Peter,' she pleaded. 'Can't you see we've no energy to waste. You can have it out with Ross when we're home.' Her voice wobbled for a moment but recovered. 'Come on,' she urged, in her most conciliatory voice, 'we need your brains now, Peter, more than ever – the things you know, how to just plain survive, all that. We're depending on those things now we haven't got anything else.'

Peter's wrath subsided. He felt no compassion for Ross, but Lou had made a point. Sheer survival was going to take up all their energy and ingenuity. His hands dropped, he turned away from his brother.

'At least we know not to depend on *him*,' he said scornfully. 'Just as well I can rely on you, Lou. The first thing now is to search for those packs. They could be washed up or snagged further downstream. Even one of them'd be a tremendous help.'

Ross stood up straight. He did not say a word or even look at the others. He just began to walk away downstream.

'Wait a moment, you,' shouted Peter, but Lou stopped him.

'Let him go, Peter. If *he* can find the packs it'll be a good thing in every way.'

'He just goes off,' snorted Peter, 'and leaves me to cross the creek twice more. We've got to collect the rope. It's about all we do possess and we can't just leave it tied to that whitey-wood over there.'

'Couldn't we just have a quick search for the packs and then come back for it,' suggested Lou, who felt she could not bear to watch anyone cross the creek again, not just yet.

'Waste of energy,' snapped Peter. 'This won't take five minutes and it's got to be done.'

Resolutely he once more put the rope round the lace-bark and tied a careful bowline.

He was wrong about the five minutes. Even with Lou helping all she could, paying out and pulling in the rope, it was nearly half an hour before the creek had been crossed and re-crossed and the rope was coiled across Lou's shoulders. Peter picked up the rifle lovingly.

'Here's something that may save our lives,' he said. 'It was the most marvellous luck that you'd just handed this up to Ross. Lucky, too, the chump didn't drop it back into the river.'

'Is the ammunition all right?' asked Lou.

Peter unwound his parka from round the rifle. Of course the rain had soaked the outside, but the contents of the pockets were dry. Peter patted the bag containing the magazine clip and cartridges.

'Very, very precious,' he said.

He put on his parka, looked down at his glistening wet legs.

'Wish I hadn't lost my jeans with my pack,' he sighed, 'there's a feast in store for the sandflies.'

They set off downstream in pursuit of Ross.

Ross was still stumbling on, searching more and more desperately for the packs. A terrible despairing feeling kept telling him that by now he had gone too far; the packs would never have floated that distance without becoming waterlogged or snagged. He refused to believe this; he just had to find the packs, or it would be his fault if Lou and Peter and he all starved or died of exposure. So he crashed on and on, tripping over roots, ducking under the twining lianas, and his panic grew.

'No food,' he was half-weeping, 'not a scrap!'

There was no trace of the packs. The creek swept by, swift and evil; the bank was a tangle of unknown horrors, dimly seen through the curtains of rain and a low mist that was gathering.

Ross suddenly gave up. He stopped running. The rain and tears ran down his face. The trees seemed to crowd in on him, he felt trapped. And terribly alone. He knew that he could not just wait there for Peter and Lou, he had to find their company as quickly as possible. He began to retrace his steps, at first slowly, still half-searching for the packs, but then faster and faster, till he was running again and calling as he ran. Surely they could not have been so far behind him?

With a sudden thud in his stomach Ross realized he could have passed them by. In this rain and this mist he could have been running along the bank while they were down on the shore. He stopped. The panic inside him was like a pain, he wanted to run and shout, but his legs had gone wobbly and his breath came in spasms. Ross flopped down on the bank and put his arms over his head to try to stop the roaring in his ears.

Peter and Lou moved slowly and systematically downstream. Peter had no faith in Ross, who could easily have failed to spot the packs. It seemed reasonable to suppose they would find at least one of them. But, in fact, they never did. Presumably the whirlpool had sucked them down or somehow the straps had become entangled in a snag below the surface. Anyway all three disappeared and were never found.

As the mist thickened, Lou became anxious about Ross.

'Where has he got to?' she kept asking uselessly. Peter did not answer or even care much. In the mist and rain it was all he could do to keep scanning the banks.

At last the moment came when they had to give up. They just could not see the far shore any more. The rain was easing off a bit but the mist was dense. Peter reckoned that, especially without food, they ought not to get over-exhausted. It was about five o'clock, but already, with the mist and the darkness under the trees, there was that hint

66

of evening when thoughts turn to finding shelter; and to food. A grim moment when you have neither.

'I reckon we'd better stop and shake down for the night,' said Peter. 'What's the matches situation?'

'Your's and Ross's were in the packs,' answered Lou. 'I've got mine all right. One box. But, Peter, we can't just forget Ross. We must find him.'

'He'll have to find us,' said Peter, 'no point in everyone wearing themselves out chasing round after each other in circles.'

The way Lou looked at him made him momentarily ashamed of his harshness and he added lamely, 'A good fire'll guide him back. And warm us all up. We need cheering up.'

'I'll say,' agreed Lou. 'I wish we'd had a tin of something for lunch instead of an Oxo cube. It'll be a delicious brew of plain hot water for supper. The creek's so thick and brown here we'll pretend it's soup.'

'You won't, you know,' said Peter. Lou looked up quickly. He really was being snubbing; every remark she made was wrong.

'Well, I will even if you can't,' she maintained.

'I only meant,' said Peter, 'the billies were strapped to the packs. We've nothing that can hold water. So no hot water and no creek soup.'

He had begun to cut twigs with his knife, taking great care with each one, notching and fraying the wood to make it catch fire easily. There was no dry wood yet again, no axe even to chop for heart wood. Peter was trying to remember all the tricks he had ever learnt to get a fire going with wet kindling.

Lou's stomach was rumbling at the thought of food, or rather of no food. She was determined to ignore it.

'I'll collect up fern leaves and beech branches for us to bed down on,' she said, 'so we aren't lying directly on the wet earth.'

67

'If you could make a pile of them somewhere,' said Peter, 'I'll try and get this fire going and heat up stones and dry off a patch of ground. I've read about this dodge. Then you move the fire and the stones and sleep on the warm patch.'

'That's a good idea.' Lou was impressed. 'Oh, I do hope Ross finds us. He'll be so wet and cold and he hasn't got any matches.'

They both worked away for about half an hour. Peter whittled dozens and dozens of sticks, stuffing them into the front of his parka as he did so, to keep them out of the rain and warm them up a bit. They both collected dead bits of fern and plenty of branches and stacked them at right angles to a big boulder with a bit of overhang. Here they had laid a flat bed of stones on which to light the fire. With luck the stack would shelter the fire and the fire would dry out the stack. At last Peter built a little pyramid of whittled sticks, and crouching over it to keep off the rain, he struck one of Lou's matches. Lou put her hands around Peter's to shelter the flame. They held their breath as the match flickered feebly, then part of a twig began to smoke. Another flared up for a moment, then subsided.

'It's going out!' cried Lou.

Peter grabbed the handkerchief which Lou had wrapped round her match box and ripped off the hem. Tenderly, almost, he held it edgeways against the smoking twig. The cotton caught fire and glowed. Peter crumpled it under the pyramid and gently blew on it. With each breath, out and in, it lived and died, red and black. But at last it lived and breathed spirit into the wood shavings, which began to crackle. Peter dropped on bits of fern, more twigs; the flames grew. For another half hour Peter stayed on his knees, tending and coaxing and feeding the little fire. Then he stood up and grinned at Lou.

'She'll be right,' he said.

Lou took over the job of caring for the blaze, building it up bigger and bigger. Peter rolled three rocks together to make a second fire-place near by. When this was built he and Lou began to move the fire over to this new site. They dragged the half-burnt logs, raked the burning brands with forked sticks and scraped the embers along with stones. They burnt their fingers and at one point nearly let the fire out, but Peter was ready with more tempting slivers and shreds and soon the flames were rising bravely against the big stones which threw the heat forwards. Still they worked on, now moving the hot stones that had been under the first fire-place. Once sure there was no danger of sparks on that patch any more, Lou and Peter sat on it, hunched under the overhang in their parkas. The firelight flickered on their faces and warmed and dried and cheered them. They both tried so hard not to think about food that they thought of little else.

'I wonder where Ross is,' sighed Lou for the hundredth time.

'We've got to sort out some problems, Lou,' said Peter, ignoring her remark, 'not very pleasant thinking but it's got to be done. We've really only got our brains and common sense to save us from, well, everything.'

He did not say the word 'death', though he had intended to, quite casually. Lou knew death was all around them, in their hunger, in the cold and wet, in the dark vastness of the bush.

'Brains and common sense,' repeated Lou bravely, 'well, I've never noticed we're particularly lacking in those two things. We've got your sheer knowledge too; I'd never've got a fire going with one match in this set-up. Or thought of drying a patch of ground to sleep on. We've got the rifle. And there must be edible berries and ways to snare birds and catch fish.'

'Good old Lou,' said Peter with affection, 'you've really got guts. Most girls'd sit down and cry.'

'I don't think they would,' said Lou honestly. 'I've

heard that girls are great survivors when they're really up against it.'

'Funny to think some people choose a situation like this on purpose,' said Peter. 'They get themselves dumped on an island or disappear into the wop-wops just to get away from it all. They do it from choice, and they make a go of it. Come out years later with beards down to their knees and after a week decide they don't like civilization and want to pack off to the bush again.'

'Well, it'll take some time for me to grow a beard down to my knees,' smiled Lou, 'or you either for that matter. Let's count our blessings, shall we? There's the rope and the rifle and ammunition for a start. I've got the box of matches and the remains of the hanky.' She was rootling through her pockets. 'There's my note-book and pencil, Cop's map. And my penknife and whistle.'

'Whistle!' cried Peter. 'What are we waiting for?'

He grabbed it and began to blow. The sound came out loud and clear, slicing through the confused roar of wind and rain and creek.

Dot dash dot, dash dash dash, dot dot dot, dot dot dot, he blew.

'What's that?' asked Lou. 'Nearly SOS but not quite.'

'It's "Ross" of course,' said Peter, and blew it again. 'Ross may only know half the Morse code but I bet he knows his name. They're all easy letters too.'

With a stick he scratched the dots and dashes on the ash-strewn ground for Lou to follow, though by now it was so dark she could only just see what he had written.

'There you are, Lou; keep blowing that. I'll have a look through my parka pockets.'

Lou did so. With each blow she prayed that Ross would hear the whistle or see the fire. She pushed away the thought that Ross, trying to reach a pack, might have lost his footing and followed it into the creek.

Peter had the five cartridges, safe and dry. There was also his knife, a strong stainless-steel one.

70

'We could signal with this on a sunny day,' he said, 'it's very shiny from rubbing in my pocket.'

He wore a wrist-watch. He had no other assets.

'I put all my bits and pieces in the outside pockets of my pack,' he sighed. 'I haven't even got any Poof for these poor bare legs of mine.'

It was quite dark now, or it seemed so to Peter and Lou, because their eyes were accustomed to the bright fire-light and everything else was in shadow. In crannies under rocks or in hollow trees tiny glow-worm lights shone like little lamp-lit windows, seen from very very far away. Lou handed the whistle back to Peter.

'Your turn again,' she said.

A voice spoke from behind them.

'Don't bother, thanks all the same,' said Ross. 'Hello all.' He had control of himself. There were going to be no histrionics or tears of relief.

Lou jumped up in welcome, pulled Ross up to the fire. Peter scarcely looked at him. He threw another branch on the flames and said:

'Oh well, now the kid's back we might as well get some sleep.'

CHAPTER SIX

THAT night seemed interminable. They curled up on the dry patch and to begin with, while the fire was high, it was not too bad. But the rain never let up and the wind direction changed a little, blowing the rain and the smoke against the big boulder, so that the overhang no longer kept them dry and the smoke obliged them to get up and gasp for breath away from their so-called dry patch which grew damp again as soon as they were no longer sitting on it. Sometimes they crouched close to the fire, drying out in front and scorching their faces while the rain drummed on their backs. After a while they would turn round and their backs steamed dry while their faces were lashed by the rain.

Ross was the only one to fall asleep reasonably soon, utterly exhausted, mentally and physically. When the smoke blew over him he coughed and growled and pulled his parka hood over his nose. In his sleep he cried out and kicked Peter, which did not improve Peter's rest. He was trying to think and plan. The first thing was to stay alive. That would take all their time and energy. They must scavenge, hunt, set traps, build shelter. No good trekking on and on looking for X. They must find a decent site, not in bush as dense as this and above the danger level of the creek. Later, when they were fed and fit, they might climb to the tops and look for the lake or arrange some signal fires. There was no hurry. Three weeks. They *must* stay alive.

Peter's mind refused to think about what might be happening to Cop. He tried to make plans to find food.

Roots, perhaps, as well as berries. He knew a lot of the native berries were poisonous, tutu for instance, and ngaio. Must not take risks. He thought of how to make traps for birds or possums. Would possums live in such deep bush? Cop had asked them to look for possums but he had seemed to be sort of joking about them. There must be plenty of edible things around. Peter could almost smell roast meat and hot gravy; his mind kept getting back to the subject of eating. He lashed out at Ross, who was spread across at least two-thirds of the dry ground. Poor old Lou was still awake, hunched up in the rain.

And so the long hours crept by and sleep did not come. At about two or three in the morning the rain stopped, but the interminable wait for dawn dragged on. As first light began to etch shadows from the darkness, Peter thought: 'We'll move on when we can see well enough for safety. In about half an hour.'

That was when he suddenly fell asleep.

Lou could see his calm face as the sky lightened. She envied him and Ross. She lay watching the bush come alive in the early dawn. Trees loomed up, patches of shadow seemed to hover. She saw a giant bird with a hooked beak, waiting like a vulture. 'Only a tree-stump,' she told herself and turned away. Suddenly all round she seemed to see prehistoric creatures, a million million years old; a dinosaur swayed its head, hump-backed monsters watched her from every direction. As the dawn rose the shadows changed. The dinosaur became a giant wave about to break and dash them all to pieces. The bird became a totem pole with evil faces carved one beneath the other. She shut her eyes and refused to let herself watch any longer. She listened instead to the bell-birds ringing in the dawn and to the squeaks of fantails and riflemen. These sounds were beautiful and familiar and she felt comforted.

Ross woke about an hour later and that roused Peter. Lou sat up, glad to find the monsters had gone and the bush was just bush in the daylight. She began to rub her feet, which were numb. It was the first time she had ever stayed awake all night and she felt almost proud of herself. Peter did not believe her.

'You were snoring like a trooper at one point,' he said, but Lou felt certain he was wrong. Anyway, they were all

Scale-like lichen
fungus (orange)
rotten blackwood
Shaggy moss
Logs at dawn

awake now and wishing they had some breakfast to cook on the last embers of the fire.

Lou filled her pockets with the odd ends of dry wood littered round the outer ring of the fire. Ross wandered about, doing nothing in a way that maddened Peter who was trying to concentrate on the rifle. The trouble was, he did not know how to load it. He had done some target shooting with a ·22, but a ·303 was not a ·22, and shooting to provide food for the family was a very different affair from firing on a range. He felt distinctly apprehensive about it.

He looked up to see Ross munching and offering a stained handful of something to Lou. Peter leapt up.

74

'What's that you've got? What are you eating? Don't touch it, Lou!'

'All right, all right,' mumbled Ross, 'we don't have to ask your permission for everything, do we? Just giving Lou some breakfast as it happens. No one's asked *you* to eat it.'

Lou hated being pinned between Peter's officious care and Ross's kindly ignorance. She tried to be tactful.

'I was just going to show you what Ross has found,' she said. 'You really have got sharp eyes, Ross. Look, fuchsia berries, Peter, they're all right, aren't they? Good to eat, I mean?'

'Delicious,' said Ross, dribbling slightly. The purple stain ran down his chin.

'You ought to do the bite test,' said Peter, 'no one but a complete ass'd just rush off and eat the first berries he found. You ought to hold one in your mouth and see whether it burns at all or tastes bitter. Then after a good ten minutes you can swallow just one.'

'I know,' said Ross, 'or rather I can guess. Then you wait ten hours or ten days to see whether I get sick or die. And if I survive and you're not dead of starvation by then you'll deign to eat some yourself, if you can find any. Life's too short. I'm hungry *now* and when I'm hungry I eat.'

He thought of clutching his stomach and pretending to vomit, but Lou looked so worried he decided not to tease her.

Peter's hackles were up.

'I'm talking good sense. What's the use of planning how to keep us all alive if you go right ahead and poison us?'

Ross interrupted.

'I'm only offering Lou fuchsia berries, which we've all seen native pigeons gorging on in the past, loving every one and not, I repeat not, turning up their little pigeon toes afterwards.'

'Actually I do think fuchsia's all right,' said Lou, 'though you are absolutely right in principle, Peter, and I

75

wouldn't dream of eating anything I didn't recognize without the taste test. But fuchsia's safe, surely?'

Peter mumbled something about unreliable people making mistakes on which other people's lives might depend. He pretended not to notice the berries Lou had put down beside him. His stomach rumbled in anticipation of food; he was ashamed of its tactlessness.

'Well, let's get going,' he said. He slung the rifle across his shoulders. Ross picked up the rope. Lou carefully gathered up the fuchsia berries. They might not find any more and this was the only actual food they possessed.

They set off downstream, glad to be on the move again and work off the stiffness of that awful wet night. All the birds in the bush were singing fit to burst, as though they too were throwing off the memory of the storm.

After half a mile the creek came out of the gully that had confined it and spread itself across a broad bed, shallow, except in the centre, and running more slowly. Presumably it flooded widely in this area, there were no big trees and the ground was very boggy and treacherous.

Peter led the way, jumping from tuft to tuft. If they had been full of breakfast and energy it would have been fun, but it was an exhausting procedure; nothing was amusing under the present circumstances.

Suddenly the sun appeared over the mountain across the creek. At once everything came awake and began to warm up, as suddenly as if an electric current had been switched on. The children's clothes steamed, the sandflies came out to feed. A thin bird call whined across the bog and there was the sound of wings as two ducks flew low over the water.

'Shoot, Peter,' jeered Ross, who knew quite well that Peter was not at all certain how to load the rifle.

'I think they were blue duck,' said Lou, 'they're terribly rare and strictly protected.'

'You're always allowed to kill for sheer survival,' Peter said.

76

On they went. The ground began to slope more steeply and the bog drained into the creek. They squelched through the mush and emerged on the gravel edge of the creek, where walking became quite easy for nearly an hour. It was just as well. Lou found her legs were going wobbly. It was a peculiar feeling. She had great trouble in making them walk and had to think hard about each step. It was hot now, too, and the sandflies were delirious over the good meat provided by the children's unprotected skin. Peter's bare legs were the greatest attraction. The sandflies swarmed so thickly over them that he might have been wearing black tights. He gritted his teeth and refused to complain, but sometimes the itching was more than he could bear and he would plunge into the creek and kneel down. Thousands of sandflies would drown, but thousands more would swarm aroung waiting voraciously for their breakfast to re-emerge.

Once when he did this, Peter saw an eel whip away from almost under his feet. He made no comment. It was too cruel to describe seeing a meal swim away. He kept thinking how unwise it was to be pressing on like this, scaring everything with the noise of their approach, instead of quietly camping and stalking food. If only they could find a decent open camping place, safe from the creek.

The slow miles went by. Lou was having more and more trouble. She kept thinking, 'I'll have to tell them soon I want a rest,' and then coaxing herself on with imagined situations. 'Just the length of our drive and then I'll tell them,' she thought; and, when she had accomplished that distance, 'Suppose I were crossing some frontier to safety somewhere. This is no-man's-land, I mustn't give in till I reach the other side.' She stumbled on more and more slowly. 'I'm going up the aisle in church,' she told herself, 'I can walk that far – I'm going to be married,' and she tried a thought or two about the young man waiting at the chancel steps but could not raise any enthusiasm. Sandflies intruded on her imagination. 'Wish I'd got a wedding veil right now; that'd keep them off my face and neck.'

Suddenly the ground shelved up and hit Lou. Lou was grateful to it. She lay quite still and through half-closed eyes watched the trees reeling over and away behind her and the sky spinning through space while a blob in the middle was rushing in and out of focus saying, 'Lou, Lou, are you all right?'

She was perfectly all right, but too tired to find the words to say so. She shut her eyes and let herself fall blissfully asleep. Lou was always sure this was what happened, but she never confessed to the boys. They believed she had fainted and she saw no reason to argue the point. After all, you are unconscious, whether you are asleep or in a faint. But she always felt a bit guilty about it.

She woke, or 'came to', in quite a short while; it is hard to stay asleep, no matter how tired you are, if some well-meaning person is slooshing handfuls of water over your face.

Peter was slooshing. Lou smiled at him because he looked so concerned. She began to sit up but Peter's face immediately whirled out of focus again.

'I want to sleep,' said Lou, and did.

Peter and Ross looked at each other.

'Give her an hour, then,' said Peter.

'Two hours,' said Ross, more to disagree with Peter than for any particular reason. 'I'll fish.' He sauntered off downstream, wondering ruefully just how he was going to do this without even a piece of string or a bent pin. He could guess what Peter would say if he suggested unravelling part of the precious rope. Anyway, Ross did not want to mention it. He wished he could forget that rope.

Peter shrugged his shoulders. There was no point in making any suggestions to Ross. Lou was asleep, oblivious at last of sandflies as they partook of her for lunch. Peter tried fanning them off with a branch, but it was useless.

He untied his parka, which was slung round his hips, and first removing the bag of ammunition from the pocket, covered her hands and wrists. He shaded her partly from the sun with the branch, stuck in the gravel. Then he moved back upstream with the rifle. He simply had to work out how to use it.

It was not a bit like a ·22. To begin with he could not even open it. 'Some sort of safety catch, I suppose,' he thought, 'the ·22 has one, but not like this.' He fiddled around until he discovered the catch, shoved it forwards with his thumb and was able to draw back the bolt. He peered down the barrel, then closed it again and rested the butt against his shoulder. He had heard that ·303s had a devil of a kick. Perhaps he had better fire lying on his stomach, as he had on the school range; he might not be able to control the kick if he were sitting or standing and he had no intention of breaking his collar bone.

Then he opened the rifle again, took the magazine clip and the ammunition out of the plastic bag. He learnt the trick of loading the magazine and how to clip it in. He also discovered that when he pulled the bolt back for the second time with a full magazine, a cartridge ejected rapidly over his shoulder and he spent the next five minutes looking for it in the bush.

He spent nearly half an hour practising until he was quite certain that he knew how to handle the rifle quickly and safely. Then he packed the bits back into the plastic bag and slipped the safety catch on the rifle.

Ross had not gone far downstream. He watched his brother covering Lou. When Peter went off upstream with the rifle, Ross returned. From his pocket he took a half-used tube of Poof. He measured out half an inch of the precious contents on to his finger and then very gently bent over Lou and rubbed it across her forehead. Lou stirred but did not wake. Ross smoothed the cream around, squeezed out a little more and smeared it under her chin and round her neck. He could not have his sister eaten alive, but he was dashed if he would give Peter any for his big legs.

Ross screwed the cap on tightly and stood back watching for a minute or so. He was pleased to see the sandflies were bamboozled up to a point. He wandered off then, to look for anything to eat or anything that would do for bait for fishing.

He had nothing for a hook. He put his mind to possible alternatives. Make a hook out of bone or something; bob for eels with worms, if he could find any: spear with a forked stick: or construct a trap. The more he thought about it, the more he preferred the last idea. Once built, a trap could be used again and again and would even fish for them all night as well as all day.

Ross prowled around looking for bendy twigs that would be suitable for weaving. He had in mind a sort of crayfish or lobster-pot affair, with a funnel entrance.

He cut some lacebark shoots and tried soaking them in the water to make them pliable. They would do for a start, as ribs for his basket; he needed something more supple for the actual weaving. Supple? Supplejack, of course! He dived into the bush again and began yanking at the lianas and vines that were looped around the trees.

Soon Ross had himself properly organized. He sat in the ground in a circle about eight inches in diameter. Then he wove the vines, in and out, round and round. It took quite a while but Ross was neat-fingered and he made a good strong basket. He wove it about eighteen inches high and then bent the ribs over and tried to make a decent finishing-off edge. Several of the canes snapped and Ross wished he had used supplejack right through, instead of the lacebark. It did not matter too much. By now he had his trap well planned. This was to be the outer basket. Next he would make a smaller one to fit inside it, tapering to a narrow hole at the bottom end. The eels would squeeze through this, Ross hoped, into the outer basket where the bait would be set. Then, according to fish rules, they would be unable to relocate the narrow hole in order to escape. The baskets would be sewn together with vines at the wide edge.

He pulled the stakes out of the sand, bunched them together and wound them round with supplejack. His basket was cornet-shaped. He inverted it on his head to act as a sunshade while he began to stake out the smaller basket.

A shadow fell across his work; Peter was looking down at him.

'No fish?' asked Peter.

Ross sensed an edge of criticism in his voice and retaliated with 'No duck?'

'No,' said Peter, 'and no *hat* either.'

Ross felt that if Peter could not identify a perfectly good eel trap when he saw one, there was no reason to enlighten him. He said nothing. Peter went on:

'And no Poof.'

So that was the trouble. Peter had smelt the Poof on Lou. Ross sighed and waited for the sermon about sharing everything.

But Peter was silent. Looking up, Ross could not recognize the expression on Peter's face. At last Peter said:

'Ross. I think it's because we're hungry. It does things to you, real hunger.'

Ross knew it had cost Peter quite a lot to say anything even approaching an apology or a peace offering. But he could not yet bring himself to meet Peter half-way. He pretended not to get the point.

'I'll say it does,' he said lightly, 'makes my stomach rumble like fun.' Then he relented slightly and added, 'It's a fish trap, actually,' before he bent again over his work.

Peter seemed about to protest, but then changed his mind and marched off back to Lou.

Half an hour later they were on their way once more, Ross with one basket still on his head, the other, not finished, furled carefully and wound around with some particularly supple supplejack that he wanted to use. Lou felt much better for her sleep, but not at all energetic. She trudged along apathetically, wondering how long she would last this time.

As it turned out she need not have worried. They had only travelled about another half mile when they came upon a small tributary creek, running out into the big one. It was only a trickle, easy to cross. Just beyond it the ground rose steeply for twenty feet, then flattened out into a triangular spur of tussocky grass, high enough above the two creeks to be safe from flooding, backed and sheltered by the bush.

They all stood and looked at this place. For the first time since the disastrous river crossing they all agreed without any arguing. They knew a perfect camp-site when they saw one.

'Now all we've got to do,' said Lou flatly, 'is make a camp. And all we've got to make it out of is – nothing.'

Peter could cope with camp-building even if he could not cope with hunger or his younger brother.

'We'll soon make something out of nothing,' he said confidently, and began pacing up and down the grass. 'Suppose we build bivouacs here' – he pointed along the bush margin – 'and have a huge fire in the centre here. Then we'll gradually stockpile firewood in shelter belts; protection between us and the southerly could be a blessing.'

'Whatever you say,' said Lou, past caring about southerlies and stockpiles.

'Then we'll dig at least two good holes for Maori ovens, to roast things in and –'

'*If* there's anything to roast,' said Ross; and added, to get his bit in before Peter started bossing him around, 'so I tell you what I'm going to do first. I'm finishing my eel trap and setting it in the stream. If we wait for Peter to shoot something we'll wait a week.'

He turned his back on the others and ran down to the gravelly area where he could stake out his basket again.

Peter looked at Lou.

'How do you feel? Can you help break down branches? We need masses and masses. I wish we had that axe.'

Lou set to work like a patient animal, dragging the branches, mostly beech, out of the bush as Peter hacked with his knife and broke them down.

She put the biggest ones for the bivouac, springy ones for bedding; everything else was firewood. It was hard work and Lou was worn out in no time. Peter noticed her white face and set her to an easier task, lighting a fire.

Lou sat down gratefully and began whittling sticks as Peter had done the previous evening. She produced the dry kindling from her pockets too and soon had enough to build a cage of twigs over a base of stones. The first match was successful. The fire crackled healthily and Lou went on building it up and building it up until there was no danger of its going out. One thing worried her; suppose the Boss or Boozer spotted the smoke and came for them after all? In the end she consulted Peter about this.

Peter threw himself down on the grass, glad of an excuse to rest. The moment he stopped moving about the sandflies gathered again, but Peter was getting used to them and scarcely noticed.

'Well, we've simply got to have a fire,' said Peter, 'it's just too bad if a wisp of smoke gets up to mountain height and isn't mistaken for cloud.'

'But suppose they come,' persisted Lou, 'suppose *now* suddenly a roar and they're coming hovering in to land?'

Peter nodded. 'Yes, we ought to have a plan. Do we stay or run? What do you think?'

'Run,' said Lou. 'After all this I don't want to get captured.'

'They'd feed us,' said Peter.

Lou's chin went up. 'Give us half a chance and *we'll* feed us,' she said with sudden spirit.

Peter gave her a beaming smile. 'I feel exactly the same. Just tempting you. We run. I think we run up the tiny creek, all together. We'd have a few minutes' start and they'd have the dickens of a job finding us in this bush if, for instance, we each swarmed well up a big tree and hid up there among the ferns and creepers.'

There was a sudden movement and a high-pitched squeak from behind them. They swung round to see Ross, looking rather flushed and hiding something feathery in his hand. Blood ran down his fingers.

'I have to have bait, don't I?' he began defensively.

'What is it?' asked Lou. 'What have you caught?'

'Pounced on a rifleman,' said Ross, 'and wrung its neck. But its head came right off.'

'A rifleman!' cried Lou, suddenly taken off her guard and nearly in tears. The riflemen were such tiny birds, so trustful, and Ross had betrayed one, pulled off its head.

'Don't get steamed up, Lou,' said Ross uncomfortably. 'Look, I promise I won't make a habit of it. First fish I catch I'll keep the guts for bait. But I have to start with *something*. I've tried digging but worms simply don't seem to live around here.'

Peter got to his feet and went back to cutting wood. He knew Ross was justified, but he knew too he could never have done that. He was desperately ashamed about it, but he always felt sick when he saw blood. Just seeing the blood oozing through Ross's fingers did for him. He now admitted to himself that he was terrified of having to kill a deer. Such a big, vital animal. There would be a lot of blood in a deer.

Ross went down to the creek to set his trap. He had fitted the smaller basket, which had turned out looking rather like a lampshade, inside the mouth of the larger one and fixed it securely. Now he baited the trap with the mangled bird. He waded into the creek and submerged the trap and added some heavy stones as weights. The problem was whether to have the mouth facing upstream or downstream. He decided an eel would be coaxed inside with the help of the current, so he fixed it with the entrance upstream.

For a minute or so he stood still in the creek, staring into the yellow water, flowing, flowing away behind him till he almost felt he was rushing upstream himself. Suddenly a black streak insinuated itself across the current, like a snake. Ross dared not move. It was an eel. It was food. It was going to swim into his trap before his very eyes. Ross watched. This way and that it circled the baskets, hovering, not at the entrance to the baskets, but downstream, poised against the current, unable to reach the bait. Ross saw he had made a dreadful miscalculation. The scent, or whatever-it-was, from the bait, floated downstream; the eel was longing to go in for a guzzle but had not the sense to enter from upstream where there was no scent to lead it in. Ross was in despair; such a beauty of an eel too, it looked nearly four feet long.

Ross looked round for inspiration and there stood Lou at the water's edge. Ross called her name in a husky whisper.

'There's an *eel* here,' he whispered. The eel took no notice; it did not seem able to hear him. 'Forked stick,' mouthed Ross.

Lou's face lit up. She got the message at once and also seemed to realize that Ross wanted to try to catch the eel without telling Peter, so there would be no jeers about incompetence if he should fail. Lou ran off and was back in no time with a long stick which had a deep narrow fork at one end. Just what he needed. He managed to reach it as Lou stretched out to pass it to him. Slowly he manipulated it into position over the eel. The question was whether to stab suddenly from above the water, or to submerge the stick gently and then give a final short thrust. He decided on the latter. Gently, gently, he insinuated the stick into the water. The current made a fuss and a pother getting round the obstruction but the eel seemed off its guard. Slowly he brought the stick over the head end of the eel. Stab!

'I've got it!' squealed Ross. 'Come and help, Lou, quick!'

Thrashing and plunging, the eel did not take at all kindly to being pinned down; it was rapidly gouging into the sandy bottom of the creek, determined to escape.

Lou rushed into the water.

'Step on it,' cried Ross. 'No, hang on to the stick. I'll go down and grab it.'

He took a deep breath, plunged under water, grabbed the slithery creature where it was pinned down, groped towards its head. Lou, holding the stick, was also trying to step on its wriggling tail, but that was impossible. She could not see what was going on under the churning water. Suddenly Ross's face emerged, very bright pink.

'When I tap the stick, let go,' he gasped, out of breath. 'Can't pick it up while you're pinning it down!' and he disappeared again under water on his hands and knees.

Almost at once came a sharp rap on the stick. Lou lifted it and up came Ross again, water splashing in all directions as the eel flayed around in his grip. It was all Ross could do to hang on. Lou grabbed him to steady him, almost dragged him out on to the bank.

Peter had heard goings-on and ran down from the bush to see what was happening. There stood Lou and Ross, both with two feet firmly on the eel, which somehow still managed to writhe about on the grass.

'Knife,' puffed Ross, and Peter gave him his. Ross bent down and swiped off the eel's head. Lou removed herself quickly.

'It's dead but it won't lie down,' said Ross, trying to hide the triumph in his voice.

'Reflexes,' said Peter, wishing there were no such thing.

Lou, too, was looking the other way. She knew what happened when you chopped an eel into pieces, but preferred not to watch. She could imagine it still wriggling under Ross's feet. But she resolutely refused to consider

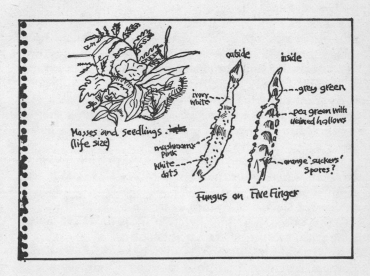

outside inside

ivory white

grey green

pea green with veined hollows

Masses and seedlings.
(life size)

mushroom
pink

white
dots

orange 'suckers'
spores?

Fungus on Five Finger

the eel except as meat, and as soon as Ross said she was no longer needed, she hurried off to the fire, to rake out a place to cook the three equal-sized pieces among the hot ashes.

It was almost unbearable, waiting for the fish to be cooked. The smell of baking was so tantalizing they could only sit and drool; it was impossible to work. Lou took out her note-book and pencil. She drew a rifleman which was hopping merrily about a nearby five-finger tree, up and round and down again, head first. Its thin squeak reminded Lou of its murdered relative, but she put that thought from her mind. Surviving was going to mean killing. If lives had to be lost, they were not going to be Peter's or Ross's or hers. She drew the five-finger too, easier than the bird; it had fungus on the underside of each leaf. The page filled up with spindly pencil lines of leaves and grasses. In the bush the bell-birds were chiming ceaselessly, like silvery dinner-bells.

Lou got up and poked the eel with a stick. Tender ... well, tender enough.

'Come and get it,' she said, but Peter and Ross were already there. Each of them spiked a piece about nine inches long. The eel seemed to have shrunk in the cooking. It was marvellous to eat something hot. They ate it as though it were hot chestnuts, burning their fingers, peeling off the skin, blowing to cool it down. But it was gone so quickly. They sucked clean the curiously shaped bones, licked their fingers and finally ate the skin separately.

It took about ten minutes for the food to have any effect on them. Then, quite dramatically, they all began to feel more benign.

'Gosh, I feel better,' sighed Lou.

'All we need now,' said Peter, 'is more food.' He added gallantly, 'That's a good trap, Ross.'

Ross stood up. 'Well,' he said, looking in Lou's direction and receiving a big wink from her, 'well, actually, I think I could modify it a little and make it better still.'

He took the raw eel head for bait and waded back into the creek, and fiddling with the trap under water, got it turned round and the entrance facing downstream. Another eel would help out with dinner. Perhaps he could catch lots, think up a way of smoking them to preserve them.

Peter and Lou were now starting to build the bivouac. First, with supplejack, they tied poles together in a tent-like shape, then they laid beech branches across the framework. Ross watched for a bit, then wandered off to a young beech that Peter had tried, and failed, to break down. Ross took out his knife and worked away at the trunk, about five feet above ground-level.

'What are you doing?' asked Lou, wishing he would give a hand and stop being so independent.

'Making another bivouac,' said Ross. 'Can't all fit in yours.'

This was true – both Peter and Lou had inwardly realized that somehow their shelter was coming out smaller than they had intended.

Peter straightened up and bit back the scornful remark that sprang at once to his lips. On second thoughts he admitted to himself that Ross's type of bivouac might be quicker and easier to construct than the conventional one he and Lou were making. All he actually said was 'Humph!'

Ross had nearly hacked through the trunk. He grabbed the tree above the cut and with all his strength tugged and strained at it till it cracked and split, without breaking clear. Ross pulled the top down to the ground. Then he ripped off the branches on the inside. His hut began to look like a wigwam, or another fish trap.

Peter and Lou had covered their framework thickly with branches and now were weaving supplejack in and out, wearily thatching the branches with an outer covering of fern leaves. Ross was soon at the same ploy with his wigwam. The work seemed interminable. No one had any energy.

However, an hour or so later both bivouacs were reasonably weatherproof, stuffed with dry bedding. The camping-place looked almost home-like, the fire blazed merrily. But a home is not a home without food.

It was Lou who said it.

'Oh, *gosh*! I'm so hungry.' She lay back in the shade of the bivouac and put her hands on her stomach. 'It really aches, doesn't it?'

'Well I thought right from the start we ought to find food even before building shelter,' chipped in Ross.

89

'That's why I did the eel trap first. Hang on, I might've caught another.'

He jumped up to go and look. Peter took Ross's remark as an accusation.

'Blaming me, are you?' he flared up at once. 'Who lost the food and the shelter in the first place anyway?'

Ross pretended not to hear. Lou said nothing. It seemed to Peter that Lou was somehow siding with Ross now, because of one wretched eel trap, whereas Peter felt that

Knock Knee effect front view

Forked tail

Beltbird
head up / down /
flicks / turns,
never still —

✔ upright legs like black wire

Bush robin

he himself had done ten times more in terms of decision-making and sheer hard work than Ross had.

Ross was coming back, thumbs down. Peter swallowed his anger, tried to be rational.

'Never mind,' he said. 'Next task; get our brains creaking on a food campaign.'

'Shoot a deer,' said Ross at once.

'Obviously,' said Peter, 'but there's not much hope in broad daylight. So until dusk let's find other things. Food doesn't have to be meat or fish.'

'The heart of a cabbage tree,' said Lou listlessly, 'if there were any cabbage trees here.'

'Aborigines in Australia eat witchety grubs,' said Ross. 'Who's for a caterpillar or beetle? Shall we snuffle under some rotten logs?'

Lou made a face. Peter took the suggestion seriously, began to lecture.

'It's no good being prejudiced. Food is just calories and vitamins and things. We don't have to enjoy it. Just stoke up a bit. I know, what about eggs? Anyone seen any birds' nests? That wouldn't be bad, omelette with hu-hu grubs instead of mushrooms.'

'Mushrooms? Fungi!' squeaked Ross. 'I know, I've heard those big flat cardboardy ones are edible. I saw some of those. Now I come to think of it, any fungus without gills is edible. Toadstools are the chancy ones.'

'Or lethal,' added Peter. 'I've thought of something else; watercress.'

'You can eat seaweed,' said Lou unhelpfully.

'Cockabullies and crayfish under the stones in the creek,' went on Peter.

'What I fancy,' said Ross again, 'is a big hunk of roast meat. Venison.' He had noticed that every time he mentioned venison, Peter became ill at ease, so he was making a point of bringing the word into the conversation as often as possible. 'Or I wouldn't say no to roast pigeon or roast duck. Something I can get my teeth into.'

'Perhaps we could make bird traps,' suggested Lou. 'Oh, I know; bows and arrows. Why not?'

'Good idea, that,' said Ross with enthusiasm. 'I tell you a bird that'd be easy to catch and that's a weka. If we put something shiny out, when it starts to get dark, and make interesting noises, I'm sure a weka'd come. They're so inquisitive. I'll make a noose and put, say, my knife in the middle. Hey presto! Catch the weka by the leg.'

'I'm wondering still about possums,' said Peter. 'We keep talking about being in such deep bush, but you never know. Just round the mountain there could be a lake with holiday cribs or a hunter's camp. There might even be a tramper's hut quite close, with stores of tinned food.'

He longed for a big tin of corned beef. He had reproached Lou for flinching at the thought of grubs and

beetles, but compared with the awful mess of killing a deer, well, a ready-cooked tin of something did sound deliciously clean and wholesome.

'Come on, all of us,' said Lou wearily, 'let's get going. I'll look for berries and fungi and a cabbage tree. And I'll turn over a rotten log or two to please Peter.'

'I'll go down to the creek,' said Ross. 'Shopping list includes watercress, crayfish, cockabullies, and in my spare time I'll make me a bow and arrow and shoot you a duck.'

'Well, I'll have a go with the rifle,' said Peter, 'we just might be lucky. I want to see if there's a deer track near the creek or anywhere that'd be worth watching at twilight. I'll look for nests too. Meet back here in about an hour and then we'll set up some nooses and traps before nightfall.'

As dusk fell and the night birds began to call, the three of them sat wearily by their fire and ate all the food they had been able to find. The big flat fungi Lou had collected were very tough indeed, even roasted, except in places where they had gone completely rotten. However, the children chewed away at them and spat out the extra-cardboardy bits. Two tiny cockabullies that Ross had caught in his hands were divided into three equal half mouthfuls, and quite a lot of fuchsia berries were heaped in three equal portions. No comments from Peter. They drank lots of water.

Ross had made a good bow and now was trying to flake a stone to use as an arrowhead. He knew that Red Indians used obsidian or flint, but he did not have anything like that. Maoris used bone for bird spears. All he had were the eel bones, which did not seem to be the right shape for anything except an eel.

Lou was plaiting strips of papery fuchsia bark. Her idea had been to make a string in which to tie a slip-knot for a snare, but it was not working very well. In fact it was not really as efficient as the thin creeper Ross had looped into a noose and staked into the ground. His knife, which lay in the middle of the noose, glinted in the firelight. Peter was telling them about the place he had found down-stream where it looked as though deer sometimes went to drink. There were no recent slots but a faint deer path led to the water's edge and he reckoned that would be as good a spot as any to –

Peter never finished the sentence. Out of the corner of his eye he saw something moving in the shadows. Care-fully he turned his head to look. Lou and Ross quietly moved till they could see too. They need not have bothered to be so cautious. The weka that strolled out of the bush seemed quite at home in the camp. It walked towards them like an inquisitive hen, craining its neck and tilting its head, examining them from every angle. Every few steps it stopped and fossicked in the ground with its strong claws, then approached once more, with naïve curiosity and never a thought of danger. It walked up to Peter's foot and gave his boot a stab with its long beak. The metal tags on the laces took its fancy and it began to

peck at them. Lou gently slid her hand to her pocket and pulled out the note-book and pencil. As she watched, she drew. Ross was so hungry he could hardly bear it.

'Grab it, Peter,' he whispered, wishing he were closer; wishing it would inspect *his* boots. Peter heard the urgent whisper but pretended he had not. There was something disarming about the fearlessness of this bird. It had never met a man, nor had any of its forebears. It did not know that men kill to eat. It was still in the Garden of Eden stage of existence. He wondered how long he would feel like this; how hungry he would have to get to strangle a tame bird. He had never seen a weka so close before. 'Not *this* weka,' he thought. 'Perhaps if there are lots of them; another evening, not now.'

The weka was simply asking for trouble. It left the safety of Peter's boot and caught sight of the gleam of Ross's knife. Eagerly it ran to look. It put its head right down to the knife, it prodded it with its beak. Ross, who had been lying on his stomach, began to creep towards the noose. The weka looked round at him in a friendly way. Ross got his fingers over one end of the creeper. The weka put one big scaly foot right into the middle of the noose. Gently, Ross began to pull. The circle grew smaller. The weka looked down, pecked at the noose and moved it right over its own toes. Ross yanked the creeper tight and the next instant he was sitting there holding the bird against his chest. The weka looked surprised but above all interested in Ross's shiny metal shirt button. It began to peck at it, stabbing Ross's chest by mistake once or twice.

At that moment another weka appeared from the shadows. It almost ran towards Ross. Peter and Lou began to laugh. The ridiculous creature did not want to be left out of any adventures. It clambered over Ross's knee and scrambled up his thighs towards the shirt button. The two birds stabbed this button joyfully together. Ross was thoroughly disconcerted.

'Anybody actually got an appetite for weka right now?' he asked, holding the button out towards the birds, so that they could enjoy it without puncturing his skin too frequently.

'Well, no . . .' said Lou.

Ross chuckled. It was such a ridiculous anti-climax to the care with which he had set his noose.

'I suppose Peter'll say I'm soft-hearted,' went on Ross, 'but I'd like to let these chaps go free. If they're as simple as this to capture, just by flashing my magic button or your enchanted bootlaces, we could always get one any evening we were desperate.'

'Oh yes,' cried Lou at once, 'it'd be too awful to kill one of a pair like this. With the other watching.'

'And Peter's going to get us a deer at dawn,' went on Ross, not to miss the opportunity of a dig at his brother.

Peter seized the loophole.

'Oh well,' he pretended to grumble, 'if you two are ganging up together, it doesn't make any difference what I say.' Then he began to laugh. 'It'd be like eating Tweedledum and Tweedledee. A real comedy team, these two.'

So Ross undid the slip-knot, and in due course the wekas hopped off his lap, a little disappointed because they had not managed to steal the button. Lou made a last desperate scribble at her not very successful sketches as the birds stalked off into the shadows. Peter watched them go rather grimly.

'It's a fine alternative,' he thought. 'A deer in the morning or a weka tomorrow evening.' He hoped that hunger would get the better of his scruples, because scruples or no, Lou and Ross must be fed. His stomach gave a terrific rumble at that moment, as though adding, 'Don't forget me! I need feeding too.'

CHAPTER SEVEN

PETER woke several times in the night, afraid of over-sleeping. He would listen to the moreporks calling out their names; to the weird shrieks which came, perhaps, from their friendly wekas, or perhaps from the most secret of all birds, the kiwi. Then he would drift asleep again and wake a little later. As soon as he sensed the sky was growing lighter, the stars paler, he crept out of the bivouac he was sharing with Lou and stirred up the glowing ashes of the fire. Thank goodness it was not raining. Peter pulled some more wood across the embers and warmed himself. It was going to be horribly cold, lying still waiting for dawn; he might as well start warm. He zipped up his parka, then turned his attention to the rifle. Everything must be ready; he could not risk making a noise once he was in his hiding place. He loaded carefully, put a round in the breech and then slipped on the safety catch. Quietly he left the camp and set off downstream.

A bird was calling across the creek; it sounded more like a puppy yelping than a bird. Perhaps *that* was one of their wekas. Peter reckoned he would rather shoot a deer in a proper hunter's way than take advantage of a tame bird and wring its neck.

It suddenly occurred to him he ought to test the direction of the wind, in fact he should have done that first of all; the deer could have already scented him and been scared away. He licked a finger and held it up. The result was reassuring. The wind was blowing quite strongly upstream towards the camp. The deer tracks crossed the stream at right angles; unless the wind backed or veered his scent would not blow across that path.

It was still almost completely dark and it was with difficulty that he located the exact spot where he had planned to lie in wait. He shivered as he lowered himself on to the damp ground. At least the sandflies would not be biting in the dark. He hoped the deer would come before the sandflies did or he would never be able to keep still.

He lay on his stomach, watching where he knew the deer track came down to the creek. It was too dark to see the exact place. His eyes felt blurred, shadows seemed to loom and disappear, to thicken and then melt away as he stared at them. He tried to tune his ears to listen for the tap of a hoof on stone or the crack of a branch, but the burble of the creek so close muffled other sounds. Only his own heartbeats throbbed in his ears. Every now and then his stomach gave strident rumbles which he could not stop. 'If you don't shut up you'll frighten away your breakfast,' Peter told it. He noticed how thin his wrists seemed to be after only three days without a decent meal.

Imperceptibly the sky lightened. He found he could now see the far side of the creek. If a deer came it would look like a shadow, like that bush beside the water. Peter's heart gave a leap. The bush was putting its head down to drink. Now he could see it clearly against the water. Every moment the dawn was creeping up on them. Any moment the deer might get wind of him or finish its drink and go away. Then Peter realized there were two deer, perhaps a third. Now it had got to be done. He was thankful he could not see the animal too distinctly. Very carefully he raised the rifle, pressed it into his shoulder to control the kick. He looked along the sights and aimed at the deer's head. He had a feeling that hunters aimed at the heart. He reckoned that at this distance a shot into the head could not fail to kill it.

Peter took very careful aim. The first deer had finished

drinking and was standing still with its head held high, while the other deer bent to the water. Tensed for the kick, Peter squeezed his finger on the trigger and fired.

The explosion was shattering; shock waves seemed to rock the whole valley; reverberations were hurled back and forth. Peter immediately reloaded. He could not see whether he had hit the deer. Then he saw a dark shape sprawled by the creek. He jumped up, rifle in hand. He suddenly remembered the danger of a loaded firearm. So he slipped on the safety catch, propped the rifle up against a tree. Then he ran towards the deer.

As he did so there was a crashing behind him and for a moment Peter thought more deer were coming at him.

It was Ross.

'Terrific, Pete!' cried Ross. 'Simply terrific!'

He had forgotten yesterday's hostility in the excitement of the moment and the triumph of the kill. Peter was still trembling from the explosion but he grinned at Ross and together they went right up to the deer.

'Well, it's dead all right,' he said, thankful that the killing was over and had been so clean. 'I think I hit it square on the forehead.'

'Gee, it might be only stunned,' cried Ross, 'you should've aimed for its shoulder. I've heard you can stun a big animal like this and when you take your eyes off it for a moment, it's up and away.'

'All right!' shouted Peter, 'you know everything, don't you.' He felt suddenly furious with Ross. 'Go and get the rifle if you want to; fire a shot yourself, waste another cartridge. Don't you know a dead deer when you see one? Look at it!'

They did; luckily. The deer was scrambling up on to its hind legs, shaking its head. With a yell Ross leapt upon it and the deer toppled sideways, struggling.

'Kill it, Peter,' screamed Ross. 'Use your knife; quick, it'll get away; cut its throat!'

Peter already had his knife in his hand. Then his nightmare was upon him, his secret dread. In the dawn light he could now see the animal all too well, a young buck, with terrified brown eyes, nostrils dilating, its mouth, its tongue, muscles quivering down its sleek throat. All the time Ross was crying, 'Quick, I can't hold on for ever. He'll get away!'

Peter stood still, sick with horror. Ross was astride the animal holding its head back by the ears. Suddenly he got a glimpse of Peter's face. Ross at once knew for certain what he had always suspected: Peter would never kill.

He took command. 'Give me the knife,' he ordered, and blindly Peter obeyed. Ross yanked back the deer's head with his left hand and with his right hand plunged the knife savagely into its throat. As the blood spurted Peter began to vomit.

Almost at once they heard Lou's anxious voice.

'What's happened? Are you all right? What on earth's going on?'

Ross shouted back immediately; the last thing he wanted was for Lou to see the massacre; it was not a pretty sight, nor was Peter.

'Go back, Lou,' he managed to call, 'everything's fine. Peter's shot a deer. Go and see to the fire.'

Ross felt marvellously elated, everything was coming right at last. Slowly Peter turned to look at him, unable to believe his ears. 'Peter's shot a deer' – that was what Ross had said; not 'I've killed a deer'; not 'Peter's lost his nerve.'

Ross grinned at Peter and crossed one bloodstained forefinger over the other. It was a secret sign they had used since they were both little. Peter understood perfectly. It was the sign of a secret treaty. Ross's bowline was to be forgiven, ransomed by the killing of the buck. Ross would never tell.

Peter raised his hands and crossed his fingers too, to ratify the treaty. He would never mention bowlines again.

'Forget it all, Pete,' Ross said gaily; 'you *did* shoot it. I just finished it off. Come on, how do you feel about the next stage, turning dead deer into venison steak?'

'Queasy,' admitted Peter, able at last to speak the truth.

'Well, I'll start,' said Ross. 'I'd just as soon no one watched my efforts. Perhaps you ought to help Lou dig a pit to make a Maori oven?'

'Ross,' began Peter; 'I want to –'

'Me too,' interrupted Ross. 'Let's forget. Okay?'

'Fair enough,' grinned Peter, and went to wash in the creek before going back to the camp to do the digging.

Lou had already made a start.

'How the Maoris ever did this,' she puffed, 'without a decent spade, I can't imagine.'

'I can,' said Peter. 'They chose softer ground. Come on, Lou, I'll do it. Only let's find a better spot.'

So together they went nearer the creek and began to scrape and scoop with such sharp flat stones as they could find. Lou kept asking about the deer and telling Peter how clever he was, which was embarrassing.

'Forget it,' he kept saying, 'Ross has got the worst of it. Jolly decent of him to offer.'

Ross was, indeed, having trouble. He had never seen an animal skinned or cut up and could only guess how to go about it. He slit the skin down the backbone, pulled it apart and was cutting strips of meat from the deer's back. Flies by the hundreds had arrived to join him.

Peter now had a tidy little pit about two feet deep and wide and long. Lou had piled lots of stones round the fire and in the embers. These were getting very hot; she kept turning them as though they were cakes that had to be cooked evenly on every side.

At last Ross emerged from the bush downstream, carrying dripping chunks of meat.

'Best steak for breakfast!' he called, 'though it'll be lunch-time before it's cooked. I thought you could make a start with this and I'll have another go and see if I can cut some joints later on. The haunches shouldn't be too impossible.'

'That's marvellous,' said Lou, examining the meat with a housewifely eye, 'four big steaks each. That should keep us going for an hour or so.'

Peter stamped on a long stick and cracked it in half without snapping it right off. With this he began manoeuvring hot stones from the fire into his pit, holding the ends, one in each hand, and rolling the stones along downhill. Ross and Lou helped. Over the stones Lou laid leaves, then they all scooped up handfuls of water and splashed the leaves which hissed and steamed. On top of the leaves went the meat and then another really thick layer of leaves was laid on top of that. More water, more steam, and then they scooped earth back over everything and filled up the hole. The Maori oven was complete. All they had to do now was wait – for about four hours, but with the certain knowledge of a good meal coming to cheer them on.

Lou watched with pleasure as she saw Peter and Ross amble into the creek together, bend over the eel trap, and then, chatting amicably, wander off downstream. It seemed their tempers had improved and she was thankful. She herself turned up the little stream that joined the main creek just above the camping site. She did not intend going far, but felt she wanted to know the territory round the camp properly. At the back of her mind was the idea of finding somewhere to hide if the Boss and Boozer came back.

The morning was ringing with bird song. The chiming notes of the bell-birds rang from every side. The little grey warbler sang its plaintive song and flicked about the undergrowth. She could see the semi-circle of white on its tail. That song had always been one of her favourites, a sad song in a minor key, yet with a gleam of hope in the ringing finish to the trill. In the distance she could hear 'Kee-a, Kee-a,' and could imagine the big parrots wheeling round calling out their names to the valley below. 'Kee-a.' She had often seen keas; in fact, once one had perched on her father's pack and ripped it with its strong curved bill while he was looking at plants up near Mount Cook. She knew they were bronzy green on top and had scarlet under their wings. She was not so sure about their close relations, the kakas. People said kakas could mimic even better than keas and could copy any noise you cared to make, that they were born clowns. They were much less common than keas. Lou had always wanted to see one.

After about ten minutes Lou sat down and began to sketch. Whether it was the temperature or whether after so many bites she had become immune or distasteful to sandflies, she did not know, but they were certainly less of a menace now.

She tried to draw the bigger trees; what were they? Kahikatea; white pine? It was terribly hard to tell because every big tree was draped in parasites, ferns and mosses and orchids, all tangled up with other climbing plants. Twenty different leaves could be counted, but the true leaves of the actual big tree grew high up above the lower leaf canopy, almost, if not entirely, out of sight. She lay back on the moss and stared straight up. Tiny birds in a flock were playing way up there, parakeets perhaps, or bush canaries. She tried to write down the sounds. 'I'll look them up when we get home,' she thought; 'if we get home,' she added in all honesty.

Lou sat up again and stared at the bush all around. She remembered how threatening it had seemed two nights before, how terrifying. But now there it was, just existing, as it had for thousands, millions of years before any man or any animal had ever set foot there. New Zealand was a country that belonged to its plant and bird life, a paradise for them. Lou realized she herself was probably the first human being who had ever seen these actual trees. She felt herself to be a speck in size, a flick in the ticking of time and the passing of centuries.

At the foot of the big tree she had drawn there was a hole. It was draped over with creepers and she only noticed it because she was trying to draw these. It occurred to her that the tree might be hollow. That if she could squeeze inside and find room there to sit or stand, it

would make a very good hiding-place in case of emergencies. So she went to look.

Down on hands and knees she peered into the hole. It was inky dark inside. She put one arm in and waved it about; there seemed to be plenty of room. Dare she try to crawl inside? Something might be living there already and pounce. Then she smiled at that fear. There are no dangerous animals in New Zealand; no snakes. She just might meet a kiwi, nose to beak, and what could be more exciting than that? Lou ducked her head and began to wriggle through the hole.

The bole of the tree must have been about five feet in diameter. The hollow part was not nearly as wide as that, but there was certainly room for someone Lou's size to get comfortably inside. She scrambled up on to her feet and stood still, letting her eyes get used to the darkness. Above her head a thin ray of light came in through a small hole. At her feet a stream of light passed in through the way she had entered. Once she was accustomed to the lighting she could see the inside of the tree quite well. The hollow chamber was about three feet six inches across at ground level and tapered as it rose up to the speck of light, twelve feet up. Above that was darkness. Plenty of ventilation; rather a strong smell of damp wood; and – Lou wrinkled her nose – there was some other smell, something acrid; she had never smelt it before. She bent down and peered into the crevices at ground level. A nesting kiwi? No such luck. She looked up again. And blinked. Something was falling like soft rain on her face, only it was not wet; something dry. Lou held up her hands to catch some of the whatever-it-was. It was powdery stuff. She rubbed it between finger and thumb. Powdered wood? Did living trees have borer beetle? Then she heard a movement from up near the hole and another fall of powder went down the back of her neck.

'Something at home, up there,' thought Lou. 'I mustn't frighten whatever-it-is.'

She made a soft, croaky, friendly noise, but the whatever-it-was did not answer. There was a faint sort of settling-down noise; whatever-it-was was getting itself comfortable. Very lightly, something else floated down and landed on Lou's nose. She managed to catch it – a feather, but she could not see it properly.

In one hand she now held some of the powder, in the other this feather. So it was with some difficulty that she

bent down and manoeuvred herself out of the hollow
tree. It really was a very good hiding-place. Lou sat down
against a tree-fern outside and examined what she held in
her hands.

Yes, it was powdered wood, sort of flaky, some of it. The
feather was roughly greenish yellow; more precisely, the

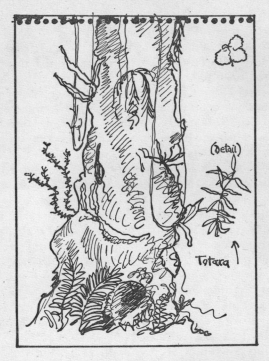

(detail)

Totara

tip was green, then came a patch of brownish yellow and
then more green. Lou put both finds between the pages
of her sketch-book and began to walk back towards the
camp. There seemed to be a very faint pathway, not a
track, just a sort of line that had been trodden down. 'Perhaps the wekas came along here,' thought Lou, picking
her way through the vegetation. She tried not to use the

pathline herself, not wanting it to show up if the tree was to be her hiding place.

Back at the camp Peter and Ross were sitting side by side, almost hidden in a cloud of flies – bluebottles this time, not sandflies. Peter looked up at once.

'Oh, there you are!' he exclaimed, and Lou realized from the tone of his voice that he had been slightly worried about her absence.

'I just explored a bit up the little creek,' she explained. 'What are you doing?'

'Nothing much,' said Ross. 'I've put two haunches of venison and assorted chunks under those branches over there. But I don't know. I just want to eat really. We haven't done anything except play at butcher's shops.'

Peter was fiddling with a strip of deerhide, scraping it without much interest, though the bluebottles were helping enthusiastically.

'We were just talking about the effects of being starved,' he said. 'At the moment all I want to do is sleep. Until the meal, I mean.'

'What's the time?' asked Lou, who knew that sleepy feeling very well. 'Wonder how that meat's getting on?'

'About another hour to go,' said Ross.

Lou lay down. She wanted really to tell them about her hiding-place and everything, but she had used up all her energy. Nobody talked. The three stomachs kept up a rumbling conversation but that was all.

Lou must have dropped off asleep. Ross woke her up by smacking his lips in her ear.

'Lookie Cookie!' he was saying. 'Dinner-time! Lay the table, polish the silver, fetch the wine.'

Lou sat up, astonished to find how far the sun had moved to the north.

Peter was already unpacking the oven. They all helped, carefully scraping off the earth with curved pieces of bark, shifting the hot stones with stick loops. Marvellous smells of baked meat rose from the pit.

Gingerly they removed the last leaves which covered the steaks. There lay the meat, looking too delicious for words, though a fraction sandy, but who cared about that? They each spiked a large steak; for a moment looked at each other in glorious anticipation.

'For what we are about to receive we *are* truly thankful,' said Lou, and they all began to eat. It was the best venison steak in the whole history of cooking; tender, done to a turn, juicy, and lots and lots of it. They ate, at first rather fast, then they settled down to a steady munch.

'S'funny,' remarked Lou at the end of her third large steak, 'I know Man is called omniverous and I always like fruit and eggs and cheesey things best. But when you're really hungry, meat's the stuff. We're carnivores at heart.'

Ross made tigerish noises and began his fourth steak. Half an hour later they were all in their bivouacs, having first managed to find just enough energy to put one haunch of venison on to more hot stones at the bottom of their oven and pack that down properly for the next good meal.

'It really was wonderful of you, Peter, to shoot that deer,' murmured Lou sleepily. 'You too, Ross, to do all that cutting up and everything.' She felt full and benign.

'Well, thank you for cooking it,' said Ross handsomely.

'You know what?' said Peter, changing the conversation. 'This adventure; it's starting to be *fun*.'

Then like three sated lion cubs they fell asleep.

CHAPTER EIGHT

PETER was right. The adventure was starting to be fun – food made all the difference. Then too, Peter and Ross had stopped their quarrelling. Lou never knew why, but she noticed the difference and was thankful. Everybody's spirits rose. None of them doubted that eventually Nick would find them. With food and shelter, it seemed certain that they could stay alive for many weeks. The struggle to survive had changed magically into a camping holiday.

Late that afternoon, after a long sleep, Ross found an eel in his trap. He killed it and that evening, as they sat talking round the fire, he was fiddling about with a pliant stick and some deerskin thongs, trying to invent a way of preserving eels by smoking them.

'Collecting firewood is going to be our biggest drag,' Peter was saying, 'we need stacks and stacks of it.'

They planned to have two big stores of wood, one for what Lou called 'domestic' use, the other for emergency signalling, so they would always have enough for a big blaze at night or for lots of smoke by day. To keep it dry, most would have to be stacked under a thatched roof, but some branches would be kept green and damp for smoke signals.

All sorts of plans tumbled into their heads now that the first great need for food was overcome. Lou took out her note-book and wrote a list of everyone's ideas.

(1) *Make baskets for collecting and storing berries and fungi.*

(2) *Dig pit downstream for sanitation.*

(3) *Dig another oven.*

(4) *Make arrows for Ross's bow.*

(5) *Another eel trap: test Ross's eel-smoking invention –* 'And invent a different one,' said Ross ruefully; the fishing-rod object from which the eel dangled kept falling into the fire and getting burnt and the eel badly charred.

Lou told the others about the hollow tree she had found and added to the list

(6) *Each decide on hiding-place in case of enemy invasion.*

Peter suggested inventing a code of bird whistles.

(7) *Calls,* wrote Lou, whose whistling usually failed her in a crisis. The idea was to be able to communicate with each other without the enemy realizing it.

(8) *Most important, explore territory.* Now they were in good health and spirits the boys felt it their duty to obey Cop's original orders and climb above the bush-line and search for X.

'Actually,' Peter pointed out, 'we could even be quite close to a lake with a township.'

Ross added that they might come up on a marked track for trampers or a deer culler's hut.

They had a discussion about the map Cop had drawn in Lou's note-book. They studied it carefully and then Lou made a suggestion which, to her surprise, the boys supported.

'Burn it,' said Lou, 'those men were after Cop because of X. Don't let's *have* a map. Don't let's risk them finding it.'

All three of them knew the picture by heart, all could draw it in the sand. Lou tore the page out of her book and held the paper over the flames. It twisted into a grey shadow, rose like a wraith with the heat and smoke, and the ashes disappeared into the dusk.

Suddenly a noise not unlike a ship's hooter came from up the creek, a hundred yards away.

'Shivers!' exclaimed Ross, then could have kicked himself for sounding scared. 'A kiwi?' he asked, trying to make his exclamation into a joke.

Lou frowned. She never could distinguish the night birds, except the morepork. Wekas and kiwis all shrieked. Very quietly she got to her feet.

'Must go and look,' she whispered. Peter put out his hand and gave her the whistle.

'Just in case,' he whispered back.

Silently Lou walked across the short grass, then very carefully began to go step by step along the way she had taken that morning. The shriek seemed to have come from that direction.

There was another booming noise, followed by a cheerful glugging from over her head. She strained her eyes in the darkness under the leaf canopy but could not make out any shapes. So she just stood still, stopped using her eyes and concentrated with her ears, poised to catch the slightest unusual sound. She found she could censor out the chatter and rush of the creek, the wind in the tree-tops, the crackle of the fire at the camp.

Something was climbing along a branch. She heard shuffly sounds, the scratch of a claw, the snap and rustle of twiglets. The noises were interspersed with little clicks and chuckles as though the creature were talking to itself. Lou listened and listened; instead of getting louder the sounds receded; no ... not that exactly; Lou's ears were puzzled, then came up with the answer. The creature was going up, not away.

'A possum, perhaps,' thought Lou. 'A bird would surely fly if it was going up.'

The next sound, however, was a bird sound without a doubt. There was a flap of feathers, either wings or tail, followed by a swishing whirr. Lou stood astonished. A large bird was sailing down towards her on outstretched wings. It was like a toy aeroplane coming in to land. No flapping, no fuss, just a skilful downward glide and it ar

111

rived on the ground almost at Lou's feet. It was a parrot-like creature with a large hooked bill.

It folded its wings, waddled here and there, noticed Lou and put its head on one side, then on the other, giving her a thorough inspection.

'Hello,' said Lou. 'Hello, Joey.'

The bird did not exactly return the greeting, but it made a scratchy noise, not unlike a parrot learning to talk.

'Hello,' said Lou again, letting her voice drop on the second syllable.

'*Ky-oo*,' said the bird.

'Not bad for a first try,' said Lou. 'Hello, hello, are you a kaka?'

The bird was not at all afraid. Like the wekas, it was obviously fascinated to meet an unknown creature. It stumped up and down, round and round her. It squawked and cooed and clicked and chuckled; Lou mimicked its noises and it mimicked Lou.

Lou did wish the light had been better; darkness was falling so rapidly, within five minutes the bird was no more than a shape that moved and conversed. Lou lost sight of it in the shadows. Later she heard it climbing again and reckoned she could just distinguish between the scraping sound of its claws and the scratch of its bill, which it was doubtless using as an extra crampon.

Lou looked around. But for a faint glow through the trees that betrayed the fire she would never have known which way to turn for the camp. She tried to walk back quietly, but not being able to see where she was putting her feet she was about as quiet as a herd of cows going through brushwood.

'We had our wekas here again,' said Ross. 'Only they pushed off when you came tip-toeing through the tussock. Was yours a kiwi? Did you see it?'

'Sorry to scare the wekas,' said Lou. 'At least we didn't have to wring their necks and eat them. They must be thankful for small mercies.'

'Well, was it a kiwi?' asked Ross again. 'Come on, do tell.'

'No,' said Lou, 'a kaka I think. Not a kea, the bill was different. Hang on, let me try and draw what I remember. Not that I could see it terribly clearly.'

She pulled out her book and by the fire-light tried to sketch what she had seen.

'Really, birds are impossible,' she sighed. 'It's their

chins, or rather their no-chins. How do their necks join their mouths?'

Peter leant over to look.

'Not like that anyway,' he laughed. 'That's like Julius Caesar without his teeth in – a huge Roman nose petering out at his Adam's apple. Did it really have sideburns?'

Lou giggled. 'Yes,' she said firmly, 'just like that. A most distinguished bird.'

A piercing hoot-toot came from the tree-top up the creek, followed by an imaginative assortment of noises.

'But not very gentlemanly language,' commented Ross, 'I distinctly heard a four-letter word.'

They all began to laugh and Lou put her things back in her pocket. Peter made up the fire and they went into their bivouacs, snuggling into the dry grass and leaves over a mattress of springy beech branches. They fell asleep to a lullaby of cacophonous comments.

It rained around midnight but the sun rose and put a stop to that, drying out the pools and sending twisted skeins of steam floating away up the valley. The fire was still a bed of hot ashes; they had it going in no time and tried eating the smoked eel for breakfast. It was not a happy experiment.

'I can *not* understand,' mumbled Ross, lying on his stomach and rinsing the taste out of his mouth with creek water, 'how anything could come to taste like that in less than twenty-four hours. I'd swear that'd been fly-blown for a fortnight.'

Peter was looking at the pile of branches under which they'd hidden the rest of the deer-meat.

'I'm wondering about that lot,' he said. 'Goodness knows what the rain will've done to it already, and now it's going to be a hot day with flies . . .'

'I think we'd better eat what's been cooked right now,' said Lou, 'rather than risk wasting it. Then we'll fill the oven again and that'll cook enough to see us through to-morrow.'

So once more they scraped off the earth and leaves and took out the stones and sat down to a big meat meal. It was very good haunch of venison, but not as hot or delicious as that first big steak feast the day before, when they had been so hungry that the pleasure of eating had been almost too exquisite to bear.

'You know what,' said Peter, licking his fingers, 'there's not a cloud in the sky; we're well fed and refreshed now. Let's climb this mountain of ours today and have a look over the tops and see if we can find that lake Cop drew.'

'Good scheme,' said Ross, and Lou agreed too.

Eventually they decided that the boys should do the climb and Lou stay at base camp. It was not, Peter explained, with more courtesy than truth, that Lou was not a good climber. But if they got lost or the weather changed, the safest thing would be to have someone at the camp to build up a fire as a beacon and use the whistle to guide them back. Lou did not mind. She wanted to try some of the other ideas on that list. Make some baskets, think out a possum trap, try to see the kaka again and draw it properly. She thought she would wash her clothes and swim in the creek and have a good clean up. The more she thought about it, the less she envied the boys sweating and puffing up through the bush.

So off they went without her. The parkas they tied round their hips by the sleeves. Peter carried chunks of cooked meat in his pockets and Ross slung the rope over his shoulder. They had no container, so could take no water.

When they had climbed for half an hour, they came out on a bluff which commanded a good view of the valley. Far down below they could see the camp site and Lou sitting near the creek bending over something. Actually she was trying to weave a basket like the ones from the Islands sold in souvenir shops, but there were no broad flax leaves to be found and grass was terribly hard to manipulate. Lou was even wondering whether knitting it would be easier than weaving it.

'Let's give her a coo-ee,' said Ross, putting his hands to his mouth, but Peter stopped him. 'She might think something's wrong,' he said; 'better not.' And on second thoughts Ross agreed that calling and waving could easily be misinterpreted.

Peter looked at his watch. It said nine o'clock.

'We must work this out, Ross,' he said slowly, 'and try to take some kind of bearing on where we are.'

He drew on a mossy rock with a stick, as Lou had done on that first day of flight.

'At mid-day the sun'll be due north. I know there's some way of using a watch as a compass. If I point the hour hand at the sun now' – he twisted the watch – 'no, it can't be that, or do I point the twelve at the sun? Is north half-way between the hour and the twelve? Oh, dash it, Ross, can *you* see it?'

'No,' said Ross, 'but if you turn the nine to point at that peak over there that looks like a Red Indian's nose, then the mountain that looks like an upside-down pudding basin is at seven. And the camp is about in line with that. Is that any good?'

'I'm not sure,' said Peter slowly, 'though if you hold the watch that way the sun is at three. And we know the sun is half-way between sun-up and mid-day, so three is north-east which makes the Red Indian south-west of here and the pudding basin – er – sou'sou'west, is it? The camp ... the camp. Heck! I ought to be able to think it out; honestly I am dense!'

'I wouldn't say that,' said Ross kindly, 'not dense. Just thick.'

After a short scuffle they continued upwards. The parkas were unpleasantly hot round their hips, but the weight they carried was negligible, so they pressed on at a good speed. Getting through the bush seemed easier than it had been. Whether it was their experience or easier bush they did not know.

After an hour the character of the bush changed: the trees were shorter, then bush hebes replaced trees. There was no longer a leaf canopy and the sun was hot on their heads. Then they came out above the bush-line into the snow-grass with occasional knife-sharp clumps of spear-grass. They scrambled through the giant tussock and over crags; up and up towards the skyline. They kept looking back but the view was blocked by the bush and a fold of the valley.

'Have to get right up on the ridge before we see any-thing,' puffed Ross.

'Suppose we'd better make some marker to show the way down again,' said Peter. 'A cairn, do you think?'

He realized as he said this that forty-eight hours before he would have told Ross to make a cairn, not asked him. Probably explained what a cairn was, too. Funny that business over killing the buck had changed things. He really admired Ross for what he'd done then, and also because he'd been so decent about it. Ross was a confederate now, a brother-in-arms. Simpler than that even, Ross was his brother. For the first time in his life Peter was aware that this word meant more than just an extra person around the family. He had no time to think about it right then, building the cairn, but he tucked the thought away at the back of his mind for later on.

The cairn was soon finished. They gave it some branches on top for decoration. It had a finger of stones at the base, pointing to the place where they had emerged from the bush.

They sat down then and rested and ate about half their meat, till they were both refreshed and keen to go on. Then they went straight up from their cairn to the ridge. Three times they thought they had reached the skyline but each time another higher point challenged them. The wind from the north hit them as they breasted the third ridge. For a few minutes it was marvellous to be cool after the sweat of the climb. Then both boys put on their parkas. Ross left his unzipped because of the coil of rope he carried across one shoulder and his chest.

The fourth time it was the real thing. They had reached the ridge of a long saddle that ran almost due north–south and a fantastic panorama was spread out down below. They could see for miles and miles on both sides of the ridge. The bush looked as it had from the helicopter, like a green eiderdown, quilted by the lines of the valleys. The boys scraped clean a patch of ground to use as a drawing-board, began to map their position, drawing with sharp stones. There was Pudding Basin mountain, that one must be Red Indian Nose; they were looking down on it now. So the camp must be ... Peter twiddled his watch. It was now one o'clock. The sun would be past due north. Perhaps north *was* half-way between the hour hand and the twelve if you pointed the hour hand at the sun.

'The camp must be ...' Peter hesitated, then plunged his finger on their plan. They both looked in that direction, from east of the ridge. 'See, that valley,' cried Ross, 'that's our valley, isn't it?'

'I think it must be,' said Peter. 'Yes. I say, Ross, follow it back, look' – he jumped up excitedly – 'do you see? There, where the valley divides again.'

'Wow, you're right!' cried Ross. 'That must be the Dividing of the Waters where the whirlpool was. Which is the valley we called "Our Creek"? Can you follow that one back? We might even see the waterfall and where we crashed.'

But fold upon fold of bush obscured their view. Valleys crept like wrinkles in every direction. The boys turned to examine the west side of the ridge. The mountains rolled away as far as the eye could see; presumably somewhere beyond them lay the Tasman Sea. On the brown tops the snow-grass rippled under the wind as though it were breathing. Far to the north-east they thought they could see snow on the heights, where Mount Cook and the glaciers and the highest peaks in New Zealand reached for the sky.

Ross sighed; partly for the glory of it all, but also for disappointment. No lakes, no sea, no habitation or short-cuts to civilization. Peter was looking southwards up the ridge, which like the back of a giant animal sloped steeply on both sides, yet still went uphill like the neck leading up towards the head, which lay to the south.

'Let's go up to the very top,' he said, 'we still can't see in that direction. We might be missing a landmark that-a-way.'

They set off. The wind, blowing strongly from the north, pushed and bustled them up the slope. After perhaps half an hour what looked like the very highest point of the mountain stood against the sky a hundred yards ahead.

'Race you to the top,' cried Ross and began to run. Suddenly the wind caught in his flapping parka, whipped it up over his head, ballooned it out like a spinnaker sail. Ross began to stumble, to be tossed by the wind; he seemed to have lost control of his legs.

For three seconds Peter watched, grinning, then suddenly a kind of electric alarm buzzed in his nervous system. Before he could rationalize it he was tearing after Ross. Then he knew what he feared. That topmost peak could be on the edge of a precipice; Ross could be blown clean over the edge.

Peter was wearing his parka properly, zipped up and pulled in tight at the waist. The wind blew him up the slope but he was master of his movements. He ran swiftly, strongly, faster than Ross who kept half-tripping and staggering as the air currents caught in his parka and almost lifted him off his feet.

Ross had nearly reached the summit. Peter could see he was trying to stop himself. Ross threw himself on the ground but the relentless wind tumbled him over and over. Peter tore up the last few yards and leapt on Ross, getting him at the knees in the kind of rugby tackle that puts a boy straight into the first fifteen. The wind could not roll two of them, their combined weights were too great. Ross clutched at an edge of rock and hung on.

When he could see through eyes that streamed with tears from the wind, he thought for a moment he was in a green cloud. Then he realized that the confused green mist was, in fact, bush a thousand feet below him. He was on the edge, the very edge of an almost sheer drop. He shut his eyes, nauseated by the sight; he felt the whole mountain was rolling round and round to tip him over.

He was not sure if he screamed or whether that was the wind. Something was screaming. Then he felt pain, rocks scraping his face, and after an agonizing moment of imagining he was slithering forwards, he realized he was being pulled backwards, away from the precipice. Peter had him by the ankles and was dragging, yanking him to safety. Ross went limp. He seemed to miss out some part of what was happening. The next thing he really understood was that he and Peter were out of the wind; they were in a hollow of shelter in the lee of a large rock. Peter was sitting beside him, trembling and panting. He was pointing to the south, at something beyond the edge of the precipice, something that Ross had not noticed in the terror and turmoil of near catastrophe.

'That lake!' Peter kept saying. 'Look, Ross, look at it! It's that lake. Ross? Do look. It's the lake.'

Ross looked and there was a lake, a very small lake. Then he saw an island near the edge, recognized the shape; looked for and saw a peninsula of land pointing like a finger towards the island. Neither Peter nor Ross were in any doubt. They had memorized every detail of this lake, had learnt it from Cop's map.

'Follow where the dotted line went,' said Peter, and both boys' eyes turned to the left.

'For about four times as far as the width of the lake,' quoted Ross.

Peter pointed: 'That area, that's the spot where X was marked.' He waved his hand in a vague circle. 'Nothing special about it, bush like everywhere else.' In his mind's eye he could imagine Cop's big X drawn across the green.

Suddenly Ross sat bolt upright.

'Can't you see? Shivers! I can. *Look*, Peter!'

His fear was forgotten; he sprang to his feet, but Peter dragged him down again.

'What is it? For goodness sake tell me before you get blown over again and the secret perishes with you.'

Ross grinned; 'It's our place, X marks *our* spot. Our camp is just about there. See, get your bearing on Pudding Basin and Red Indian.'

'Wow!' Peter was certainly impressed. 'You're absolutely right. We might've guessed. There'd just be room for a chopper to land at the camp.'

'And it's by a creek, Cop said that too.' Ross was laughing with delight and relief. 'Now we're safe. Nick'll find us for sure. Spot on.'

'*And*,' said Peter, 'we've got another fortnight, about a fortnight. We've found X the spot. So you know what we'll do now?'

'Too right I do,' cried Ross, 'find the other X. The unknown quantity. The whatever-it-was Cop was looking for.'

'We could've found it already without realizing it,' said Peter.

'We're camped on a gold-mine,' squeaked Ross.

'We've been heating up rocks of gold-bearing quartz for our Maori oven!'

'Gee! There could be nuggets at the bottom of that oven. Would gold melt with the heat? That second lot of venison wasn't as good as the first. Kind of metallic, didn't you think?'

They both laughed and then talked about other metals – uranium, titanium, perhaps iron sand in the bed of the creek.

Peter looked at his watch.

'One thing I know,' he said. 'Time to make tracks for home. The wind's getting worse. Clouds in the nor'west too, and that means rain.'

'Okay, time to go,' said Ross. He hesitated. 'That wind,' he went on, 'would it be ... er ... wise to rope ourselves together, do you think? I mean ...' he hurried on, 'I've carried the wretched rope all this way and your weight and mine combined were more successful against the wind than mine alone. And then I could zip up my parka properly,' he added lamely, hoping Peter did not think he was lacking in courage.

'A good idea,' agreed Peter. He raised one eyebrow and looked at Ross sideways. 'We could ... er ... revise our bowline technique?' he suggested.

For a moment Ross's face was expressionless. Then it creased into its usual smile. 'You took the very words out of my mouth!' he declared.

They moved slowly northwards back down the saddle in the teeth of the wind. They could hardly see for the wind whipping in their eyes. Neither of them stumbled or got blown over, but it was reassuring to feel the pull of the rope between them. After nearly an hour of this Peter stopped.

'Must've missed it,' he shouted downwind to Ross who was behind him.

'Was wondering that myself,' yelled Ross. 'Can't see properly. Should've put a cairn on the top of the ridge.'

'Stop *what* grid?' shouted Peter, who could hardly hear Ross at all.

Ross turned and began to go downhill. No good yelling against the wind. He led the way almost to bush level, with the wind now screaming into his left ear and all his hair whipped over to the right. Then he sat on the ground and Peter came and sat beside him. They turned their backs to the wind.

'Now which way?' asked Ross. 'I think south again. We must've passed the cairn. Should've followed the bush-line really, and not gone down the ridge.'

'I did think of that,' said Peter, 'but this scrubby stuff is terrible to walk through compared with the ground up there. But I agree, I think we've passed the cairn.'

So back they went, the wind behind them once more, nudging them into the spear-grass and rushing them over the uneven ground. Suddenly Ross tripped right over. He swore and rubbed his knee. Blood stained his jeans.

'Congratulations!' announced Peter. 'You have stumbled upon a great discovery.'

Ross squinted up at Peter, down at the rocks.

'Oh,' he drawled, trying to think up a suitable pun in reply. 'Glad I ... er ... went down well – yes ... er ... it was a wonderful trip.'

He had, of course, fallen over the cairn. Its head-dress of branches had blown away, but the pointer stones told them where to enter the bush. They unroped; then down they went and with every step found more shelter from the wind. It roared and thrashed in the highest branches, and the occasional gust whipped down the draughty corridors between the trees. Down, down, and everything grew darker in the bush and the swishing in the leaves became a drumming. The rain had come. The boys pulled their parka hoods up tight across their chins and stumbled on. To go downhill was all that mattered. In the valley would be the creek and the camp and Lou waiting for them with food and a fire and the shelter of the bivouacs.

CHAPTER NINE

Lou had built up the fire when the sky began to darken with clouds rolling up from the north-west. She ran round doing all the camp chores; checked the eel trap, which was empty; put extra stones on the branches that covered the remains of the meat store; put a pile of stones near the bivouacs in case any extra anchorage was required in the storm, and stuffed their store of dry fern into the bivouacs to save it from getting wet. She also crammed in her basket-making materials and the two baskets she had finished. One contained some fungi; the other, which had turned out to be quite strong, held a good stock of fuchsia berries which she had found a hundred yards or so beyond what she now called the 'kaka tree'.

She had just covered some thin slices of meat with hot ashes at the edge of the fire when the rain began in earnest. She dived into shelter. In no time water was trickling down her neck; the rain came in sheets and the thatch, which they had thought so thick, leaked in all directions. Lou crumpled up fern and packed it into the gaps, like Mrs Tittlemouse making her door too small for Mr Jackson in the Beatrix Potter book she had loved when she was little. Soon the roof was reasonably watertight. It did not seem worth getting soaked in a dash across to inspect Ross's roof. There was just room for three in the bigger bivouac.

She could not help wishing the boys would come back. For one thing, the rain made such a noise she would never hear if they shouted, and they would never hear if she used the whistle. Would the creek rise and flood out their oven? It was no use worrying. Lou decided to keep herself busy by going through the list she had made the day before of things to do.

Design a possum trap. When Peter had suggested it, Lou had privately felt this would be a waste of time; the chances of possums being so deep in the bush seemed very remote. But that day, as she had been picking fuchsia berries, she had noticed what looked like possum droppings on the ground and also some nibbled ferns. So she now drew a variety of nooses like rabbit snares; also one like the picture in their Brer Rabbit book with the tip of a springy sapling pegged to the ground. She wondered about the mechanics of a trap that would let a rock drop on the possum's head if the bait were waggled. Finally she was reduced to drawing a very deep pit, like a Heffalump trap, with something deliciously tempting at the bottom; perhaps a light covering of twigs over the top so that the possum could fall in but not scramble out – How stupid, possums would certainly scramble out. Lou decided that traps were not her strong point.

Her interest flagged and instead she tried to sketch from memory the kaka she had seen the previous evening. She wrote down details about it; the way it had glided to the ground; the rather stubby shape of its wings; its large size compared with what she remembered of keas, though she could be wrong about that. She still had the feather pressed between two pages of her note-book.

She turned back to the list. Baskets; well, she had made two of those. Fungi, berries; she had collected some of them. Explore mountain behind camp; that was on the way. It looked as though tomorrow would see everybody digging pits for assorted purposes and gathering firewood.

'Right now I could be thinking out this one about signal calls in case of enemy invasion,' thought Lou. 'I wonder what we'd want to say to each other?'

Eventually she decided that the most vital messages

would be 'Hide', 'Attack', 'Come Here' and 'Beware'. After some thought she jotted down an owl call, '*Hooo-oo*' for 'Hide'; a blackbird alarm note, '*Tick-tick-tick-tick*' for 'Attack'; a '*Kee-wee*' shriek for 'Come Here'; and the '*Waa-waa-woo*' noise the kaka had made for 'Beware'.

She practised them. The 'Attack' noise was the most difficult, but she reckoned it would be Peter's job to give that order and hoped he never had to.

'*Hooo-hooo*' warbled Lou, practising, two fingers in front of her mouth.

'*Hoo-hoo ya-hoo*,' came from just outside the bivouac. Peter and Ross loomed up at the entrance, blocking out the fire-light, soaked to the skin, worn out but smiling from ear to ear.

It was quite a performance getting them both inside. They took off their soaking parkas and socks; Ross had been wearing his jeans and these also had to be discarded and left at a safe distance from the fire. The boys backed into the bivouac as they undressed. Lou viewed their filthy shirts, Peter's bathing togs and Ross's underpants with disgust.

'Next fine day is wash-day,' she said firmly. 'Come on, dig down in the fern now; it's warm and dry.'

She pulled her own parka over her head and made a dash out to the fire, scraping the sizzling meat out of the ashes with the wooden tongs and rushing back with it into the bivouac.

'Gee, thanks, Lou,' said Peter. 'I mean it. First class cook-housekeeper!'

'Hear, hear!' said Ross.

Lou glowed with instant happiness.

The boys ate voraciously, burning their fingers and their tongues. Then they lay back. There was just room for the three of them side by side.

'Tell,' pleaded Lou, and so they did. Lou gasped with admiration and astonishment when they told of their discovery of the little lake and that X marked the very spot where they were camping. She made a most satisfactory audience.

'We must have a really good search round as soon as the rain clears,' she said; and again they discussed all the possibilities, trying to remember exactly what Cop had said. Lou had one new suggestion: perhaps an aircraft had crashed somewhere in the area with a valuable cargo on board.

It was an anti-climax to recount the story of her day's activities, which seemed very insignificant compared with the boys' adventures. She mentioned the four calls which she had been practising on their return. Peter approved and repeated them over to memorize them. There was no comment from Ross. He was asleep.

The storm had blown itself out by morning and the weather was fine, the sky clear. After a fuchsia berry breakfast they built up the fire again and dried off their boots. Peter and Ross then went off for fire-wood. Lou had persuaded them to wear their parkas, to keep off the sand-flies, while she gave their other garments a wash in the creek. As she stood on the shore, wringing out Peter's shirt, there was a sudden whirr of wings and three duck flew in low over the water and landed in mid-stream.

Lou dropped the shirt on the sand, groped in her pocket for her note-book and pencil. Blue duck. This time she must put them on record.

This was a family party, father, mother and junior. The adults looked the same, though one was slightly larger than the other. Both had dark slate-blue heads with a sheen of green and turquoise. Their bodies were lighter, slate-grey, glossy blue on the wings and with a dappling of russet pink on their chest. The most extraordinary part of their appearance was their bills. These were white, or perhaps palest pink, and on the tip of each was what appeared to be a huge blob of black ink, about to drip. It just did not look real, that blob. Lou began to draw; the ducks swam closer and closer, inspecting her, and they started a conversation which was so curious that Lou stopped drawing and tried to write it down.

'*Kwaa*,' said the smaller bird, in a deep growly voice, and in instant reply the larger bird stretched out its neck, lowered its head till the bill was parallel with and almost touching the water.

'*Whee-oo*,' it whistled.

Lou watched and listened, astonished. So swiftly did

the second call follow the first that, unless she had actually seen it happening, she would never have believed that the sound was being made by two birds. '*Kwaawheeoo*,' like one word. They did not call regularly but the moment the first bird gave its harsh '*Kwaa*' the other got its neck out in time for the whistle. It whistled with its bill slightly open, and sounded like a child at the learning stage, at first more blow than whistle, a heavy breathy noise, but then for a moment the whistle emerged strangely penetrating and high-pitched.

The young duck, which was dark all over with no blue and pink highlights on its plumage, took no part in the adult conversation but paddled up and down in the shallows, zig-zagging as near to Lou as it could get without going aground.

Lou was drawing again. Such aristocratic-looking birds, with Grecian profiles; the long bills sloped from their foreheads at a supercilious haughty angle. And their plumage was so sober, yet so rich in muted colours, so well valeted. Like a well-bred nobleman who finds a picnic party going on in his private property, the first duck seemed to be informing Lou with the utmost courtesy that she was trespassing, while the other added, as an aside, 'A washerwoman indeed, *wheeooo*!' But after about five minutes the three birds, surrendering to the pull of the current, floated gently away downstream, and as the creek curved out of sight Lou watched them bobbing buoyantly away. It was not until they had gone that the thought of roast duck crept into her mind. She banished it at once and hung the clothes up to dry.

The boys came back with armfuls of wood and after several journeys built a sizeable wood store, partly under the shelter of the trees. It was terribly hot wearing their parkas, but luckily the clothes Lou had washed dried out very quickly in the sun and breeze.

'Do we *have* to dig pits now?' asked Ross as he changed back into a clean, stiff shirt and jeans. 'I think we've done enough chores for one morning. Let's look for gold.'

He had a strong preference for gold over other minerals; most of all he wanted to find a nugget. It was this that prompted him to add, 'How about food next? I'll unpack the oven if you like.' There just might be molten gold under those stones.

'Actually that's not a bad idea,' agreed Lou. 'We might as well fill up on what's in there now and cook the very last of the meat from the cool store.'

Peter and Ross had to laugh. Lou's 'cool store' was a

pile of wet branches covering a loathsome heap of raw meat which looked pale and bloated by the rain. Certainly the sooner it was cooked the better. So Lou put more stones to heat by the big fire while Peter and Ross unpacked the oven. Ross was determined that there was a glint of gold in the sand at the bottom of the oven, but Peter called it 'newchum's gold' and maintained it was iron pyrites and that these rocks were not gold-bearing quartz. Lou knew that neither of the boys had a clue about geology and kept out of the conversation.

They put reheated stones at the bottom of the pit and sprinkled leaves from the pepper tree over the last of the unattractive-looking raw meat before damping the leaves and packing everything down to cook. They were running short of food again, but it was no longer a serious problem. They knew they would catch eels from time to time and it would be only too easy to grab a weka if the worst came to the worst. Or a blue duck. And they still had most of the ammunition left. Keeping meat was such a nuisance that there was no point in killing again until it was really necessary.

As they sat and ate the cooked venison, Lou re-explained for Ross's benefit, the code of bird-call signals and they all practised them, to the astonishment of the local bird population. A number came flitting and hopping down to inquire about the extraordinary noises. The practice session ended in laughter. The audience, though intrigued by the sounds, obviously did not equate them with the notes of blackbird, owl, kiwi or kaka.

'Well, that's the nearest I can get to it, Ross informed an astonished-looking tomtit.

No one mentioned digging pits. After the meal their thoughts all turned to finding whatever X was. Ross, still set on gold, was determined to think of how to pan for gold without a pan. Lou thought a decent collection of geological specimens might be valuable if she could ever show them to an expert, and she also thought she would

sketch the rock faces; the streaks and strata might be re-
vealing to a geologist some day. Peter had been thinking
of Lou's crashed plane idea. He decided to retrace the way
he and Ross had climbed the previous day, just the first
half hour of it, up to the bluff where the view had been
good and Ross had wanted to coo-ee to Lou. He thought
he would just sit there and scan the bush, section by
section, for any sign of glinting metal, scarred trees, burnt
patches of bush or snow-grass. Yesterday they had been
concentrating on landmarks and working out the points
of the compass.

'I won't be gone much more than an hour,' Peter told
the others. 'It's a half-hour climb up but it only took us
about ten minutes to crash our way down yesterday.'

Off he went. Lou chose a museum site under the trees
and began her search for samples. Mostly the rock was
grey and split easily; the sand varied in colour. Near the
creek there were pebbles, smoothed and rounded by the
rub of sand and water, and there were many different
colours, very pretty.

'I'm sure these aren't what Cop was looking for,' said
Lou, examining a beautiful rose-pink one, 'but they'd
polish up into lovely gemstones.'

'M-m-m,' said Ross, not really listening. He was
crouched at the edge of the creek jiggling with his arms.
Lou looked more closely. He was panning for gold with –
Lou nearly exploded, but what was the use? She held her
tongue. He was using his newly-washed underpants as a
pan. He had shovelled sand into them and was slooshing
this bulgy object just below the surface of the water, letting the creek current wash away the floating sand
particles as they came to the top. The theory was that the
heavier particles would sink to the bottom – Ross had tied
up the leg holes, so 'bottom' was the right word – and the
very heaviest particles of all, the last few flakes, just might
be gold. The whole family had panned for gold in Central
Otago one holiday. They had found enough gold-dust to

cover a five cent piece; the sum total of five people's efforts for a whole afternoon. Hard work too.

Lou watched Ross shaking the sand-filled pants. It looked a hopeless task.

'You could try the sand from the bank up there,' suggested Lou, pointing upstream, 'where the little creek comes out. The gold from both creeks'd wash on to that bank. Double the odds.'

'Good idea,' said Ross, rinsing out his underpants and moving up into the shade. There were fewer sandflies there too; not that sandflies were the menace they had been.

Lou was now a short way up the side creek, foraging for stones in its cool water. As her hand went down to pick one up, the water seemed to draw her fingers away from it, distorting the shape, deceiving her eyes.

So it was that all three children – Peter up in the bush, Ross on his shadowy sandbank and Lou groping in the waters of the sheltered little creek – were hidden from the binoculars that were at that very moment scanning the valley in general and the camp in particular. Ross and Lou, close to the burble of water, did not hear the distant drumming rhythm of the helicopter engine. But Peter heard it as he reached the look-out point. And he saw the chopper too, coming in from the north-east, from the direction of the crash site, hovering at the head of the valley.

For one frozen moment he hesitated, checking the code word in his head. Then he cupped his hands into a hollow and blew with all his force down between his thumbs. '*Hoo-hoooo,*' went the call; again and again he blew. Not a sign of Lou or Ross by the camp. He took his hands away and plain shouted, bellowed, the call: '*Hoooo-hoooo-hoooo,* for heaven's sake, *hooo,*' he roared, and then again he blew into his cupped hands.

Down below Ross and Lou both stood up. The hooting call had penetrated the murmur of the creek.

'There's Peter,' said Lou, 'he must've reached the bluff. I'll go and wave.'

Ross frowned.

'Don't,' he snapped, and Lou stopped short, astonished by the authority in his voice.

Ross went on: 'Yesterday I wanted to coo-ee at you. We could see you quite plainly. But Peter stopped me – said you might think it was a message or call for help. I know he wouldn't do that noise for nothing.'

'But,' faltered Lou, 'that owl noise. That means "Hide". Why should he want us to hide?'

As if in answer, the roar of the helicopter suddenly filled the valley. It was coming in to land.

Ross was across the creek in one leap. Lou led the way as fast as she could go towards the kaka tree.

'Keep off the track,' she warned.

She herself knew every inch of the way, where to jump from rock to rock, where to paddle, how to come out of the creek on a fallen log to leave no footprints in the sand. Ross followed her every step. As they were reaching the tree the ground shook and the trees trembled; the helicopter was landing. Lou dived straight into the hole and at once began to climb up inside the tree. Ross wriggled in after her. He too climbed just off the ground so that anyone glancing into the hole would see no boots and legs. Both children found reasonably comfortable niches on which to perch, propped up with their legs across the width of the tree. The only thing now was to wait.

CHAPTER TEN

IT was Peter who had to make the decisions, Peter who watched the ashes and sand whirl up as the helicopter landed; who wondered whether his warning had come in time; who watched from far above as one man opened the door of the helicopter and climbed out. With all his heart he hoped that man would be Nick or one of the organizers of the local scenic flights, a friend. It was hard to be certain from that distance. Peter screwed up his eyes. Nick was six feet tall and slim. This man was medium-sized and stocky. Peter could not distinguish his features. But he knew for certain who the person was. Boozer.

Boozer was exploring the camp. He poked his head into both bivouacs. He went a little way downstream, then reappeared on the opposite bank and came back upstream. When he next appeared from behind a tree he was holding something white. Peter did not know it, but Ross's underpants had been found.

Next Boozer got something small out of his pocket.

'Anti-sandfly cream,' guessed Peter, and grinned to think that he and the sandflies had now joined forces, attacking the same man.

'Good work, sandflies; get him! Massacre him!' thought Peter, but the next moment Boozer disappeared into the bush behind the bivouacs and Peter began to worry desperately about Lou and Ross. He felt sure they must be in the kaka tree by now. But suppose Boozer just hid and waited and watched. Eventually Lou – or more likely Ross – would venture out to fetch food or to reconnoitre.

It was up to Peter to think of some scheme and somehow let the others know what to do.

So Boozer waited and Lou and Ross waited. Peter sat and thought. His first idea was to steal the helicopter; he had watched Cop pilot a similar machine time and time again.

Cop had originally bought a dual-control machine when he had been doing aerial photography work with a fellow pilot: they had taken it in turns to pilot and to photograph. Balancing the chopper was as easy for Cop as riding a bicycle was for Peter. But that balance, that instinctive altering of lever and pedal and throttle at every manoeuvre, there was (Peter smiled, remembering a few early bicycle crashes) – well, there was a certain risk about that plan. Cop had let Peter practise each helicopter operation separately, but he had never allowed him to operate all four controls at once; Peter had never really got his balance.

Then Peter thought of contacting Lou and Ross after dark and the three of them just pushing off together somewhere else. After all, they had had no equipment since the loss of the packs; it was just the same problem of survival all over again. Or was it? No. The rifle was in the bivouac and their parkas and the rope; apart from matches, these were their only real assets; it would be crazy to try to travel with none of these.

Well, could they capture Boozer, make him prisoner, immobilize the helicopter? But someone would soon come to look for Boozer if he did not return. And then what?

Boozer went on waiting; Lou and Ross went on waiting; and Peter went on thinking. Eventually his thoughts travelled right round in a circle and he returned to the original idea. The risk would be a calculated one. If the plan was a success they would be safe, the problem solved once and for all. All the other plans solved nothing, except the immediate crisis. More dangers and risks would follow.

Peter sat and hugged his knees with excitement. The decision was made. Now for the details ...

'It's no good, Ross,' whispered Lou, 'we'll probably have to stay here till it's dark, possibly all night. So just shut up and stop fussing.'

'I'm not fussing,' squeaked Ross. 'You're the one that's fussing. I only want to slither out and have a look-see. It could be Nick or someone Dad's sent to look for us. Dad might even be with him.'

'For heaven's sake!' Lou was really losing patience. 'Use your nut. You know perfectly well that if Dad were here or anyone on our side, Peter would've been down by now to tell us. And anyway you can't *slither* out through bush; you know what a crashing it makes. I wish you'd just shut up. Anyone coming closer'd hear us whispering and we're trapped in this tree.'

'Proves you're talking nonsense,' snapped Ross. 'If what you say's true, we'd hear anyone coming crash-crash and all that. You can't have it both ways.'

Lou sighed. She herself was content to wait. She trusted Peter to do the right thing. But she had a horrible feeling Ross was going to give them away, do something impetuous, get them all caught.

'Would you like to change places or something?' she suggested. 'Only don't scare the kaka. We don't want it flapping off in a fright and showing everyone where we are.'

'No,' said Ross, 'thanks. Actually I've decided. If Peter's up in the bush there's nothing *he* can do. *Someone's* got to find out what goes on. I won't be long.'

He began to wriggle down on to hands and knees.

'Ross, no, don't; honestly you'll be caught for certain.' Lou was desperate because she knew nothing would change Ross's mind when he spoke in that voice. 'I'll come too then,' she went on, beginning to climb down.

Ross stopped for a moment.

'That'll make exactly twice the noise and we'll find out half as much. Stay put. At least Peter and I'll know where you are. Listen for signal calls. Don't come unless I call you.' He smiled quickly up at his sister. 'It's a bit like Prisoner's Base. *You* mustn't get caught, specially if Peter and I are. If that happened we'd wait for a safe moment and then signal and you'd have to dash out and free us both.'

Lou tried once more.

'But we aren't playing games now. Please, Ross. Please stay. Stay till dark at any rate.'

'So long,' said Ross, and his shoulders blocked the hole, leaving Lou in darkness. Then suddenly it was light again and Ross was gone.

He was very careful. He felt tremendously responsible. He crept on hands and feet, making for the creek. It was quieter to step over rocks than through bush, and the bubbling of the water drowned the noise of pebbles that shifted, and of splashes and slithers. He peered ahead. Nothing suspicious to be seen. Ross edged forwards with the greatest care.

Up on the promontory Peter was trying to build a fire. He had chosen the site for this after much thought. It could not actually be seen from the camp, so no one, even with binoculars, would be able to see how many children were, or were not, there. The rising smoke would certainly suggest that they were all together, perhaps cooking a meal. Peter felt sure Boozer would not be able to resist coming up to investigate. Once he had left the camp site and the helicopter Peter counted on being able to get down the hill by a different route and grab Lou and Ross from their tree, and then they would be into the chopper and up and off before Boozer could get back to stop them.

The only trouble was that he had just discovered he

had left his knife in his parka pocket at the camp, though luckily he did have matches with him. He had been breaking off branches, but it was impossible to find really dry kindling and with no knife for cutting shavings or fraying twigs Peter was afraid his fire would flare up and go out. It had simply got to be a good fire, one that looked like a cooking fire, that would go on burning lustily to urge Boozer up towards it while he himself slipped away downhill. It would be disastrous if Boozer got half-way, then lost sight of the smoke and turned back. Peter sat and ripped at twigs with his nails, peeling off the bark, putting it in the sun to dry, chewing the ends to fray them. This was going to take ages. And time was short.

Ross crept on. The trees were thinning out and he could see a glint of metal, brilliant in the sun. The helicopter seemed to be just beyond the bivouacs, towards the place where he had done the butchery. Not a sign of a pilot. Perhaps he was in one of the bivouacs. Ross tried to manoeuvre himself in order to see the make of the helicopter. Was it the enemy? Or a Forest Service one? Or one of the American commercials that worked with deer cullers?

It was no use emerging at the mouth of the creek, he would have to get into the deeper bush and work his way over to behind the bivouacs. There was a big fuchsia tree there. Its twisted branches and peeling trunk cast shadows that would make first-rate camouflage. He would climb it. Slowly he edged towards it, getting glimpses of the camp as he moved. No one near the fire. No one by the creek. He was almost certain it was Boozer's helicopter. Gee, he must take care!

He stopped for a moment, wiping the sweat from his forehead. Then he had a good look up into the fuchsia tree. For a moment he could not understand what he saw. Then, thud! His stomach seemed to drop. The curious shadows had taken on shape and meaning. Two black circles became the lenses of binoculars pointing straight at him. There were fingers holding them, a face behind; a broad-shouldered person was hitched comfortably across a branch. Boozer had also appreciated the camouflage possibilities of the tree and had chosen it as the perfect place in which to watch and wait.

For a half-second Ross's reaction was to turn and run. But he checked that. Mustn't run towards Lou's tree, or up the hill to Peter. Boozer blocked the way to the creek. The bush behind was dense. As he hesitated Boozer slithered out of the tree and came striding towards him, ripping through the undergrowth and bush-lawyer as easily as if it had been grass in a hay paddock. Ross, feeling like Hop-o'-my-thumb defying the giant, faced him boldly.

This was the moment for a commercial break in what seemed to be some fantastic television serial. But no dazzling toothpaste advertisement intervened.

'Hello,' piped Ross, more shrilly than he had intended, 'how's Cop?'

'Cop?' asked Boozer, taking a firm hold of the back of Ross's shirt.

Ross could not stop chattering.

'Well, anyway, you could call this a fair cop I suppose. Ha-ha. I'd laugh at my own joke if you'd kindly stop throttling me.'

But Boozer held on tight and began to march Ross back towards the camp. Conversation had to wait until they were out on the grass. Then Boozer asked:

'Cop? What cop? Don't care for the fuzz myself,' and as he spoke he shoved Ross into the larger bivouac and sat down at the entrance, almost blocking the hole.

'Not *a* cop. *Our* Cop. That's our uncle's name,' explained Ross, 'at least it's what Lou and Peter and I call him.'

'Your *uncle*,' said Boozer, his red face shining, '*three* of you. Well, I *am* learning a lot. Very interesting.'

As if to celebrate good news he pulled his whisky bottle out of a capacious parka pocket, drank several noisy gulps, wiped his mouth on the back of his hand, licked his hand and then settled down for a chat, the bottle conveniently within reach.

Ross had time to realize he was getting into deep water. In one sentence he had let out that there were three children involved and that Cop was their uncle. Ross was not a boy who told lies often, but his imagination suddenly became inspired.

'We were on the tops,' he began to explain, 'and we saw your chopper land near ours. Waved and yelled ourselves hoarse but you never noticed. But we saw you and your pal splint Cop and tie him to your skids and fly him out.'

'Up on the tops?' said Boozer suspiciously. 'Looked very carefully we did. Ernie's very thorough and we knew there was someone else around. Never guessed it was a pack of kids.'

'Just we three,' Ross said and let his voice gulp a little. 'Why didn't you come back for us? Why didn't you help us? Why bust up all our food?'

Boozer's voice, when he answered, was on the defensive. 'Ernie, he's a foreign joker, he's not got Kiwi standards. You can't argue with a type like that, you know. He says, in that foreign voice of his – which believe you me is more than I can understand half the time – anyway he says "Let him play peep-bo till he's hungry and then play ball." '

'So you waited – how many days has it been? I've lost count. Five at least, just to play ball with a starving child?' Ross was beginning to enjoy the sob story.

Boozer went on hurriedly, 'And then the weather broke. Can't fly in weather like that you know.' After a pause he added, 'Remarkable eyesight, you got.'

'Oh very,' agreed Ross, 'exceptional, I even watched to see if your short shaft went too.'

Boozer flinched when Ross mentioned the short shaft.

He fingered his whisky bottle but resisted the urge. Eventually he said, 'What happened to all your gear?'

'What gear?'

'Well, I searched your chopper. Taken everything, you had. Everything useful I mean; sleeping-bags and all that. But here, I been nosing around, nothing but the rifle, some rope, a parka and a pair of underpants.'

It was Ross's turn to feel uncomfortable.

'Lost everything crossing the creek,' he said, 'everything disappeared in a whirlpool. And us too, nearly,' he added, because it did sound heroic.

'Did you lose your map?' asked Boozer, rubbing his flabby nose and failing to sound casual.

'Everything,' declared Ross dramatically, 'and all the food. Not that we had much after your efforts. You got any spare grub with you?' he inquired.

Boozer edged a little nearer. The smell of whisky on his breath revolted Ross.

'Chocolate,' said Boozer, and he pulled a double-size block out of another pocket.

Ross's mouth went all juicy; he swallowed several times. Sweet milky chocolate. He yearned for it as Boozer tore off the outer wrapper, crinkled back some of the silver paper and broke off a whole row of squares with that incomparable muffled rustle and snap that chocolate makes.

He held out a large piece, four knobs, to Ross. Ross put out his hand for it with words of genuine gratitude; then suddenly Boozer popped all four knobs into his own mouth and began to munch them noisily. Brown overflow trickled down his chin. Four knobs were more than even his large mouth could hold at once. As he crunched and licked his lips he broke off four more knobs. When his mouth was empty enough to speak he made a proposition.

'You can have this,' he told Ross, 'when you've given me some information.'

'Sure, anything,' said Ross outwardly eager, inwardly gathering his wits together.

'You seen a map of round here? More of a chart, like, of a small area?'

'Course I have,' said Ross, 'though not exactly of round here. But we mapped the area round the cottage ourselves. Dolphin Sound. That's where we were going.'

'Not your Dolphin Sound place,' groaned Boozer. 'Come clean, kid. There's another area your uncle's out to explore and we all know why.'

'Wish I did,' thought Ross.

'... and *you* know where. Just you tell *where*.'

'If there was another chart,' lied Ross convincingly, 'I guess Cop's got it. We never saw it. Just followed the creek to try to get out. Perhaps it's in the map pocket in the chopper?'

'And that it's not,' exploded Boozer with great feeling. 'The hours I spent in that chopper searching for a ruddy map! "Find it," says Ernie, just like that. Then he says, "Well, find that other joker," not knowing it was three kids he wanted. Anyway, that I have done. Found you.'

'But not the others,' said Ross cheerfully.

'What's that?' said Boozer. 'How come they'd avoid me? I come to rescue you, haven't I?'

'Please may I have some chocolate?' asked Ross.

'No,' shouted Boozer, suddenly exasperated, 'you can tell me about this place your uncle was interested in. You know where I mean. I'll get it out of you.'

Ross did know where. And he was afraid Boozer might get it out of him. So he yelled back:

'I know one thing. A law about getting information with menaces. From a child too. Won't sound at all good when that comes out.' He began to enjoy the part. 'A child, lost and starving in the bush, and you wave chocolate in front of his nose, gobble it up yourself and then threaten him.'

To his astonishment, Boozer immediately handed him

the chocolate. Ross ate it at once before there was a change of policy. But he was so het up he hardly tasted it after all that.

'To tell the truth,' said Boozer, 'I seem to be having to do a lot of things I don't like in this little enterprise. I didn't know there was kids in it when I signed on. I'm fond of kids, I am.'

'I must say,' said Ross truthfully, 'you don't look the sort that takes it out on kids. Too fond of the booze. Yes. Do what Ernie says for the money. Yes. Spend the money on booze. Sure. But fix a short shaft – I bet you've been feeling pretty awful about that, specially now you know there were three kids on board.'

'Too right,' agreed Boozer, flattered rather than offended by Ross's remarks. 'Mind you, that short shaft trick was humane as you might say. The way I wrenched it. The strain of take-off finishes it, usually second or third time. So the drop wasn't likely to be more than twenty feet or so. Enough to ditch but not kill. It's a common enough way to crash if the maintenance's been poor. No one could prove anything. How did you know?'

'Well, thanks for not fiddling with the petrol feed,' said Ross, 'or we'd have been in smithereens.'

Boozer laughed. 'That wasn't in the plan,' he assured Ross, 'or the people in the know would've vanished as well.'

This reminded him of the matter in hand.

'Now this place. Be a pal and tell me about it. I been straight with you. Then I can fly you back and fix things up with Ernie. But I got orders. And I need my whisky too much not to obey them.'

'Any idea why he pays so well?' asked Ross, wondering if Boozer just might let slip what X was.

'Money's gone to his head,' said Boozer, 'like you hear happens when people win the Mammoth Lottery. He's that rich, he thinks he's the right to have anything money

143

can buy. Did you ever hear anything so ridiculous as going to all this crime – I mean time – and money just for ... here, have some more chocolate.'

'Thanks,' said Ross, accepting two more lumps. 'You were saying, just for ...'

'Well there it is,' sighed Boozer, 'people are funny. And Ernie's foreign of course. Not one of us. And I'm not to fly you out unless I get information. I'd hate to leave you behind again. Really I would.'

And Ross believed him.

'I don't see how leaving us in the bush helps in any way at all,' said Ross.

'It's a squeeze like,' said Boozer, 'and even more so now it's come out that he's your uncle and there's three of you kids involved. Ernie's pumped and pumped that uncle of yours and not a single word out of him. But he'll talk soon enough when Ernie puts it to him that your three little lives are at stake.'

Ross stiffened.

'You mean to say Ernie's still got Cop?' he asked tensely. 'You never took him to a doctor?'

Boozer wiped his nose. 'No, well, that was the squeeze, you see. Ernie reckoned the joker in the bush'd be more likely to tell what he knew if it was a question of the pilot being taken to hospital or not. Well, the pilot's your uncle. I reckon you'd feel even more strongly. And a smart kid like you can see we've got a double squeeze now. Ernie'll make a very touch-and-go story out of three little nephews and nieces stranded without food. Cop's going to tell, I think. See what I mean?'

And Boozer opened his whisky bottle and his mouth for a cheerful swig.

Lou waited and worried, and the longer she waited the more she worried, though she kept telling herself Ross was probably just being terribly careful. She did not exactly want him to hurry and take risks but she did wish he would come back. And what about Peter? How would he get in touch with her and Ross? Lou shuffled round in her narrow hiding place that was beginning to feel more and more like a coffin. Except that she had company. The kaka up in the top flat made neighbourly noises now and then that Lou found extraordinarily comforting.

'Yes,' Ross was saying, 'I do see. A double squeeze. But I want to be right in the picture. I mean, well, supposing we did know of this special area, though I'm not saying we do. But suppose we had information that'd earn our transport out of here. Where would you take us?'

'To your Uncle Cop, of course,' said Boozer.

'Where is he?' asked Ross.

Boozer shuffled about.

'Can't tell you everything,' he mumbled, 'you don't need to know *where* you'd be taken.'

'How could we be sure you'd really take Cop to hospital?'

Boozer laughed easily.

'Oh we wouldn't. You'd do that. One way or another you kids have ruined this little expedition. We'll have to clear out till it's all died down. I'll get my money, I done my bit. I'm off overseas before you contact anyone. Ernie too, in a different direction let's hope.'

'How's this work out?' asked Ross, confused.

'Simple,' said Boozer. 'Very isolated this spot Ernie chose. He'll write a little note about you to the Invercargill police and post it at Auckland airport a minute or so before take-off. Then it's over to them and you. By then Ernie'll be back in his own nasty corner of the world and I'll be somewhere else. Mind you, Ernie'll come back again. One track mind. Obsessed. I wonder,' sighed Boozer, 'what I'd do if I had all his money.'

'Drink,' said Ross.

Boozer laughed wheezily and patted his whisky bottle.

'Too right I would.'

'I'd be interested,' said Ross severely, 'to see a cross section of your liver under a microscope.'

Up on the bluff Peter's fire was laid and masses of branches now lay around waiting to feed the flames. Peter struck a match and noticed he was so tense that his hand shook as he held it, vacillating under the kindling. With his other hand he dropped minute pieces of fibre wherever they seemed needed and some strips from Lou's depleted handkerchief. The fire took a sudden hold. Soon Peter was adding bigger sticks, dragging branches across the flames. All the while he wondered how long it would be before Boozer took the bait. It occurred to him that it would be quite a good thing if Boozer got a glimpse of him, so at frequent intervals he went right out on the bluff pretending to gather fuel but also having a sharp look down for any sign of life. Whatever happened he must not mis-time this plan of campaign.

'Well I'd have to consult the others of course,' Ross was saying to Boozer in a business-like way. 'Will you please let me free so I can go and look for them?'

He made as if to leave the bivouac.

'Hey! Hey!' cried Boozer. 'Wait on, nipper. I've caught one of you and I'm not losing that one. You tell me where they are and *I'll* fetch them.'

Ross was in a dilemma. Dare he trust Boozer, give the 'Come here' call?

'You'd never find them without me,' he hedged.

Boozer took Ross's hand. Very firmly indeed.

'Out,' he said; and both of them crawled awkwardly out of the bivouac. Then Boozer gently but firmly twisted Ross's arm round behind his back in a half-Nelson.

'Now, kid,' went on Boozer, 'are you talking? And where can I find the others?'

It was at that moment that Ross saw Peter's smoke. He hung his head, hiding his face in shadow, as if hesitating

146

over the question. But really he was thinking very fast. Peter must have the situation in hand. Why should he light a fire? Boozer would be sure to investigate. This must be a plan to lure Boozer up on to the bluff.

Ross took a deep breath, as if making up his mind to speak. He looked up at Boozer, who was watching him closely, then let his gaze fix on the rising smoke for a second and the expression on his face change to one of horror. Quickly then he pretended to cover up his fear, mumbling about needing more time to think things out.

Boozer was already looking up the hillside to see what Ross had noticed.

'Ha!' he cried. 'So that's where they are. Let the cat out of the bag, haven't they, with their fire.' He chuckled.

Ross kept silent, looked away. Things were going very nicely without his saying anything at all.

'Well now,' said Boozer, 'I'll go and fetch those two.'

He stopped then and had one of his thinks.

'Now kid,' he said slowly. 'It's just occurred to me you might slip off while I'm otherwise engaged. I wouldn't like that at all.'

'No?' inquired Ross.

'No. Now don't get me wrong, kid, I've kind of taken to you. Guts. That's what you've got. But you take my point? Can't lose you. Bird in hand's worth two in the bush.'

Ross had to laugh.

'Two in the bush it may be,' he said, 'don't know that I'd class myself a bird.'

Boozer looked almost amicable.

'Well anyway, you see what I'm getting at? I'll have to make sure you don't disappear.'

The next moment Ross's other arm was also twisted up behind his back, held in Boozer's giant grip. Boozer fumbled and produced some binder twine. In no time Ross's wrists were tied together.

'I'll give you some more chocolate,' promised Boozer, 'but I have to tie you up. Your legs too, I'm afraid.'

Ross was fascinated. Gee, this was the real thing, even if Boozer was a bit on the kindly side for a proper villain.

'A gag?' suggested Ross helpfully, feeling he might as well go the whole hog. 'Oh, perhaps not. Because of the chocolate.'

Boozer made a good job of the knots.

'Going to pop you into the chopper,' he told Ross almost cosily, 'I'll put you on one of the seats. Quite snug. With the seat belt fastened. To keep you quiet, you know. Quiet *and* comfortable.'

Peter's fire was going like a bomb. A smoke bomb. He kept piling stuff on it and then dashing back to the bluff to see if Boozer had appeared. It was on one of these dashes that he saw something so terrible that he refused to believe what his eyes told him. This simply must be his imagination. But no; that was Boozer and he most definitely was carrying a body across to the chopper. And the body was Ross's. Ross was not even struggling. Boozer bundled him into the cockpit, seemed to be busy fixing something up.

Peter stood and stared.

'If he's got Ross,' he kept thinking, 'he's probably got Lou too. If he's . . . killed them, I'll . . .' He thought of the rifle. A whisper of excitement suggested that Boozer would probably fly out with Lou and Ross and leave him behind. Then he *would* have to fend for himself and no mistake.

But he was wrong. Boozer straightened up, shut the cockpit door and the next moment had his binoculars to his eyes. Peter turned instinctively and ran for cover. Then he pulled himself together and peered down through the foliage.

Boozer had certainly seen the smoke and probably had caught a glimpse of Peter too. Now he was striding along

148

the side of the creek towards the foot of the promontory. Boozer was going to come up.

Peter stood up straight, poised now and ready for battle. His hands were not shaking any more. With a last look at the well-stocked fire he began to run swiftly downhill. He reckoned it was quicker to use the route he knew for about two-thirds of the distance; Boozer's progress uphill would be much slower than his own descent. The trouble would come if they met half-way.

'No good meeting trouble half-way,' thought Peter, surprised by his own joke. He steadied his pace and hurried on more warily.

The further he went the more careful he became. Soon he was stopping every few yards to listen. The track had only been trodden three times. Boozer would make plenty of noise through the undergrowth.

At about the half-way mark Peter heard Boozer crashing along in the distance. Peter crept on another twenty-five yards, fifty yards, listening carefully, stopping every time Boozer stopped to get his breath. All the while Peter was looking keenly from side to side for a hiding-place.

'Better get off the track now,' he decided, 'mustn't take any risks.'

He began to veer off to the right, taking care to leave no boot prints in any soft patches of earth or leaf mould. It was tricky, but Peter refused to be ruffled or rash. One crash when Boozer just happened to be standing still to get his breath and the whole plan would fail.

Gently Peter got on to hands and knees, wriggled under the huge bole of a rotting tree-trunk, crawled along behind it and climbed right down into the hollow from which the roots had been dragged by the fall of the tree. There was black water at the bottom of the hole. Peter put one foot down carefully. The bottom was solid. The water was about eighteen inches deep. Peter crept right into it and sat down gently. The water came across his chest; it

149

was not really cold. He leant back behind festoons of hanging moss. The camouflage was perfect.

He waited for Boozer. Crash and stumble, nearer and nearer. Peter sat. Boozer must be about level with him now, perhaps at the place where he had left the track. Boozer stopped, swearing at sandflies. Out of training? Having a swig? Or had he found Peter's footprints? With a sigh of relief Peter heard the stumbling continue upwards.

Peter suddenly realized that as the track went higher Boozer would be in a position to look down on him from above. The big roots and the moss would hide him if he kept still, but there was no question of moving until Boozer had gone a long way further up. Precious time was going to be lost. Already Peter wanted to be bounding on downhill to find the others. But he was stuck still while Boozer laboured upwards. Boozer was going to reach the promontory and find no one there almost before Peter had time to get down to the camp and collect Lou and Ross. Then it would be a question of how soon Boozer made the decision to come down again and how fast he came. It was going to be a very near thing. Peter choked back his impatience. This was vital. He must play it right.

It took a full five minutes before the bush hid Boozer from Peter. Then at last Peter crawled out of the pool, back under the tree-trunk, and made his way back to the track. The next moment he was off downhill as fast as he could leap. By now this part of the track had been trampled four times; Boozer must be out of earshot, speed mattered most of all. Peter bounded like a deer. Within less than another five minutes he was down by the little creek.

He could see the chopper and, thank God, Ross inside it, but for some reason just sitting and doing nothing at all to help. Well, at least he looked alive. Find Lou! What on earth was the call for 'Come here'? Peter tried a '*Ki-wi*' but was so out of breath it did not work properly. Quicker to fetch her. He hurtled up the creek towards the kaka tree.

'Lou!' he cried, 'Lou, it's me, Peter. Come quickly!'

Before he had even reached the tree, Lou had heard him, was scrambling out.

'Into the chopper,' gasped Peter, 'by the bivouac. Quick! We're flying out.'

Together they ran back to the camp.

'Where's Ross?' gulped Lou, still unable to believe what Peter had said.

'In the chopper,' said Peter, 'get in too.'

'What about the rifle? Everything?'

'I'll grab it as we pass,' said Peter. 'Get your seat belts fastened. Won't be a sec.'

Within half a minute he too was clambering into the chopper, bundling in the rifle and his parka as he did so.

'Good grief,' he exclaimed, catching sight of Ross trussed up like a roasting fowl. He passed the pocket knife, which he had just retrieved from his parka pocket, over to Lou.

Ross began a torrent of excited explanations. Peter interrupted firmly, pointing out this was a time for concentration.

Peter was feeling his way around the controls. Lightly his fingers touched the cyclic stick, the collective lever, slipping back over the throttle to the starter button. His feet reached for the pedals; he pressed one, then the other, imagining the tail rotor responding to his touch. Then he ran a finger over the dials. He thanked God for a clear calm sky. Navigation would have to be by eye. The engine revs would need watching. Not much margin for error there. Presumably there was enough fuel. Boozer would have seen to that.

As the string fell from Ross's wrists and Lou sat up straight, a movement in the bush caught her eye.

'Boozer's coming!' she cried.

Peter never even looked up. He was in a private world,

listening to Cop's voice as he had so many times before. Only this time it was for real ... 'Start the engine, watch the dials, bring the revs up to at least 3,000, a little more ...'

The rotors whirled; again the sand and dead leaves danced.

'He's coming out of the bush,' squealed Ross.

'*Quiet!*' yelled Peter.

Gently he began to pull up the lever, tilting the blades to get lift. The helicopter left the ground.

CHAPTER ELEVEN

'OH!' gasped Lou as the whole machine slowly began to rotate, like a merry-go-round getting under way.

Peter knew what was wrong. Not enough left pedal. He pressed a little harder. The helicopter steadied as the tail rotor began to correct the torque.

Instinctively Peter let the stick forward a little. Balance. Just as Cop always said. The throttle needed adjusting.

'Boozer's underneath,' grasped Lou, wondering if he would bring out a gun like a television gangster and feeling at the same time that it was most rash of him to stand in such a dangerous position. She would never forget the expression on Boozer's face. She would love to draw that as soon as she could get at the note-book and pencil, still safely in her pocket. Boozer was now jumping up and down, obviously shouting and swearing. As the helicopter rose he got smaller and smaller, till he looked like an angry puppet, gesticulating and prancing on a stage with painted grass and water and crumpled-paper trees.

'Keep your eyes skinned for landmarks,' shouted Peter. 'I'm trying to go back the way we came.'

Ross nudged Lou and pointed behind them. Lou swivelled round and saw the panorama of Map Lake, the finger-like peninsula and the island. She nodded, then turned to watch ahead.

Peter tried to relax his body: being tense was no help. He remembered learning to ride a bicycle, his father telling him to lean over to steer round a corner. It had not been until Peter had learnt to relax and rely on instinct rather than instructions that he had really got his balance.

It was much the same with the helicopter. Infinitesimal alterations to this or that control made all the difference. He could never have managed at all if he had not had those dual control practices with Cop.

'You're great, Pete,' laughed Ross, who enjoyed the danger, 'she handles like a dream.'

'Wish it were a dream,' thought Lou privately, not sharing Ross's temperament. Then she caught sight of something shiny down below.

'Our valley. The smashed-up chopper!'

'So it is,' cried Ross. 'I think Cop came in through that gap to the east.'

He had to repeat that twice before Peter heard him.

Peter nodded. He eased the stick, shifted the lever, adjusted the throttle and tail rotor. Four things to do; each manoeuvre, four things, Cop had told him. It was not a matter of exactly remembering this, it was more an instinct, a feeling. Peter wished he dared take the machine a little higher in order to see further, but he knew there was a limit to the safe altitude. Cop never flew high, only of course it *was* high here because the mountains were so enormous to start with. The altimeter measured the height above sea-level. Te Anau, Peter thought, was about 500 feet above sea-level. But their camp? He had forgotten to check as he took off. Somewhere not many miles away – and how many feet down? – tourists would be crowding on to launches for the trip down Milford Sound, past Mitre Rock, out to the edge of the Tasman Sea.

Ross had taken the knife from Lou and freed his own ankles. The rough twine had bitten into his skin above his socks. He hoped it would leave even a small scar.

Peter followed an easterly course, as nearly as possible, avoiding the peaks yet keeping a reasonable height above the bush in the valleys. How far to Te Anau? Fifteen or twenty miles?

Ross was already there in his imagination. Landing;

people's faces of astonishment as three children climbed out: 'We must telephone, this is an emergency.'

Lou was feeling sick again.

As they swung up a valley leading slightly to the south, Ross gave a shout:

'Water ahead,' he cried; then, 'Oh no, it's gone again.'

But five minutes later both he and Peter saw it again.

'Can't be Te Anau,' shouted Peter, 'too far south. Manapouri perhaps?'

Ross laughed cheerfully, indicated a circle with his finger.

'Could be Map Lake.'

'Ha-ha,' snorted Peter, wishing he knew more about navigation and wondering whether people did, in fact, fly in circles, like walking in circles in deserts and bush. Next time there was any choice, he turned due east once more.

'Recognize the mountains?' he shouted at the top of his voice, but the others shook their heads.

Lou gazed down. Everywhere looked the same. Brown mountain tops, green bush, valleys, rock faces, like a relief map in the museum, painted in drab geological colours.

'We're lost,' she thought, 'lost in the air instead of on the ground. Wish we had a map.'

Map! She loosened her seat belt, bent forwards and groped behind her feet. In Cop's cockpit there was a map pocket more or less at floor level. Her fingers closed over a booklet. She pulled it out. *Playboy*, it said, and the rest of the page was a girlie picture which Lou promptly returned to obscurity. But she went on rummaging around and she found something stiffer. This time it was a map, folded back to show the right area. Boozer must have been using it too. Lou tightened her seat belt again.

Peter's attention was taken for a moment when he saw Lou had found a map. The helicopter gave a ghastly sag and he shoved up the revs. The needle on the rev counter had fallen to the lowest edge of the band that marked the safety limit for cruising speed. He must watch that counter, concentrate on the needle and keep it between 3000 and 3200 r.p.m. He left the map work entirely to Lou and Ross.

These two were poring over the map. Together they pointed to Te Anau, then to Map Lake. Lou's finger traced the route they thought they had taken. Ross pointed to Manapouri.

'We could've seen that from, say, *here*. Then we turned east.'

Lou nodded. Her finger moved on. A big mountain range lay ahead. But beyond it was Te Anau.

'Mountain ahead,' shouted Peter. 'North or south?'

Lou and Ross both pointed on the map to the North-West Arm of Te Anau. They remembered Cop had taken that route, up the Middle Fiord.

'North!' they shouted back.

'Sure?' Peter was astonished. They'd been heading east or south-east all the time. '*Sure* we don't keep south?'

'Quite sure.'

Peter could sense the certainty in Lou's voice, so against his inclination he swung northwards, readjusting everything as he turned.

Now Lou and Ross knew exactly where they were. It was all tremendously exciting even for Lou. She forgot to feel sick.

'Keep parallel with this ridge,' she told Peter, trying to pitch her voice above the engine noise. 'Follow round to the right. There's a valley. It leads through to the North-West Arm. Could be hard to find.'

Eagerly they all peered down.

'There it is!' cried Ross.

Peter gently veered the helicopter to the east once more. Suddenly there broke before them the glorious vista of the Middle Fiord leading to Te Anau lake and beyond it the familiar tops above the Eglinton Valley.

They cheered. But Peter was thinking, 'We're not on the ground yet. I mustn't make a mistake now. Must be very careful. Balance. Relax.'

On they went, and then came the moment when, looking down, they saw water beneath them instead of bush. There, on the far side of the lake, a few miles to the south, were the scattered cottages and shops and the big tourist hotel of Te Anau township. The lake was like crinkled glass. Peter reduced height and they skimmed along towards the little town.

Lou thought happily:

'If we crash now, or rather, splash, someone'll see us. People are probably watching us already.'

Her eyes went to the dials. What had happened to the fuel gauge? It marked nought.

'I'm making for the airstrip.' Peter was wondering if they would reach it. 'Tighten your seat belts. This could be a bump.'

Lou did not know whether she ought to worry him about the petrol gauge. Already he was starting to descend. There seemed no point.

'Call out the height, Lou,' shouted Peter. 'Altimeter's no good to me. I'm not certain how far Te Anau's above sea level. Guess the height.'

Lou was useless at estimating distances in feet. She swallowed her pride and did the best she could.

'Twice as high as First Church,' she shouted, thinking of Dunedin landmarks. 'Top of the spire. Station clock tower. Oh, it's not far now, about three or four storeys.'

She never noticed, as Ross did, people emerging from buildings at the edge of the airstrip, all staring up at this helicopter that was coming in without any radio communication, descending inch by inch, rotating slightly. Peter's right leg had gone all wobbly. He was having trouble pushing that pedal. He pressed hard on the floor to try to stop his foot from trembling. He took a hold of himself. One hand hovered over the throttle on the collective lever, the other was adjusting the cyclic stick. Watch that rev counter. That was better. Ross saw people push a trailer pump out of its shed. An ambulance appeared out of a garage next to the airstrip. This was really thrilling. Nearly down now.

Lou was measuring her father's height in her mind's eye. 'Three Dads,' she said, without thinking. 'Oh, I mean eighteen feet ... about fifteen ... twelve ... less now.' She caught her breath as the helicopter began to circle again. Peter's right foot was still having trouble controlling the torque caused by the tail rotor.

'Ooops, about six feet; oh Peter, we're *there*.'

Not quite ... four, three, two ... and the helicopter seemed to drop the last twelve inches, bounded once, then stood still. Peter was still concentrating. His hands moved over the controls. Switch off. Fuel off.

It was done. They were safe.

The three children looked at each other. Peter heaved a deep sigh, rubbed his arm across his forehead. Ross was chattering, eagerly unclipping his seat belt. Lou felt a great sob come welling up, but that would never do. Brushing her eyes quickly, she followed Ross out of the helicopter.

CHAPTER TWELVE

THEY had been driven to Nick's office in Te Anau. The local policeman was there and another helicopter pilot and someone from Lands and Survey. People bustled in and out bringing cups of tea and food and saying 'Fantastic! Splendid!' and lapping up every word of their story, especially Ross's conversation with Boozer. Ross had looked forward to telling a tale of high drama, but, when it came to the point, he was so afraid of letting slip anything about X that he became, for Ross, inarticulate.

Anti-climax set in. Peter was suddenly fed up with everybody and everything.

'It's not splendid!' he expostulated. 'It's terrible. We've lost Cop. He's hurt and we've no idea at all where he's got to.' He turned to Ross. 'Can't you drag up any clues?' he said. 'Didn't you get anything out of Boozer on that?'

Ross was insulted.

'Look, I found out just about everything, didn't I? He just said this place was very isolated.'

Nick frowned.

'Can you remember exactly what he said?' he asked. 'I mean, "isolated". That cuts out a lot of places. If we could pin down the area at all, I might know of a spot.'

'Well, he really did mean isolated,' said Ross slowly. 'He said we'd be left there while his boss made it for Auckland airport but he'd let the police know where we were just before take-off. So he must've meant somewhere we really couldn't get away from on our own.'

'An island?' suggested Peter.

Nick nodded.

'Yes, that'll be it. An island. Let's think. On Manapouri perhaps, away from the tourist traffic and the West Arm route. Though I dunno. People hire boats and go all over that lake. More likely one of the islands in the Sounds.'

Lou said, without thinking, 'That'd be too far.'

'What do you mean?' asked Nick.

'How do *you* know anything about it?' asked Ross, jealous of his reputation as sole information agent.

'There wasn't enough fuel,' said Lou. 'The gauge said empty about ten minutes before we landed. We were lucky to get this far.'

'Why on earth didn't you tell me?' cried Peter.

Lou shrugged her shoulders.

'Wouldn't have done any good. Only put you off.'

It was true and Peter kept silent.

'Now that's very interesting,' said Nick, 'so Boozer was counting on flying back to somewhere very isolated not as far from your camp as Te Anau.'

Lou and Peter and Ross all tumbled to the same solution at the same moment.

'You tell, Peter,' said Lou.

'Give us the map,' said Peter.

'There it is!' interrupted Ross, pointing to Map Lake and the finger-like peninsula. It was such a little lake that the tiny island was not even marked.

'I don't see an island,' said the policeman, but Nick smacked a hand down on the desk.

'There is, though,' he said, 'I've seen it from the air too. I've a hunch you're right.'

He pushed back his chair, looking at his watch.

'Just time for a quick look-see before dark,' he said to the man who was the pilot of a commercial helicopter.

Ross stood up. He felt, and looked, embarrassed.

'Um, well about Boozer. He's really a decent sort of joker and I think he wishes he'd never got involved.

160

Doesn't get on with Ernie, but he's an alcoholic. And he needs help. And he gave me chocolate.'

He looked round. Nobody seemed to be listening.

'What I mean is,' shouted Ross, '*pick up Boozer first*. I think he'll help you. He deserves a fair chance – And I like him, anyway,' finished Ross rather lamely.

Nick smiled. 'That's quite an idea, too,' he said, 'thanks for the tip. And for all the information, Ross.'

He and the pilot left the room, and after that more things went on happening, but the children were getting too tired to care. Telephone calls were made all over the place, including one to the children's parents in Dunedin. Arrangements had been made for the children to have a big meal at the hotel and to sleep there that night.

'But we must wait for news of Cop,' said Peter. 'I'm all right.'

Ross, who had dozed off, woke up and said, 'Me too,' very loudly, in case he was getting left out of anything.

'Will Dad and Mum come?' asked Lou.

'They'll come,' said the policeman, 'but not for four or five hours. And if you were my kids I'd rather find you asleep in bed than sitting up looking the way you are now.'

'Perhaps so,' said Peter, having glanced at his bathing trunks and discovered for the first time they were torn in several places. 'Promise to wake us when they come or if you find Cop?'

'Promise,' said the policeman.

He took them down the road towards the hotel. Suddenly a dark figure appeared and brilliant flashes of light dazzled them.

'What's that?' gasped Lou, but Ross knew at once. It was just as he had imagined it.

'The Press,' he whispered. 'Flash photos. We're famous!'

At that moment, blinded by the flashlights, he stumbled over the kerb.

'Poor kid,' thought the policeman, 'he's asleep on his

feet,' and with the kindest intentions in the world he suddenly scooped Ross up into his arms to carry him the rest of the way.

The press photographer took a heart-warming front page picture of that. He also got a shot of Ross furiously wriggling down again, but that one was never printed.

It must have been about midnight that the children's parents arrived. They went from one bed to the next, half-rousing each child in turn.

'Dad and Mum here, Peter. Well done, you boy! Sleep on in the morning till we wake you. Everything's under control.'

Peter scarcely heard but fell back contented into a dreamless sleep. Ross mumbled about Boozer and was told he had already been picked up. Lou caught hold of her mother's hand and fell asleep holding it, as she had sometimes done when she was a very little girl.

It was not till after ten in the morning that Lou, Peter and Ross were all woken up, properly this time, by their parents' voices. Their father was almost laughing, he had the morning paper under his arm. Their mother seemed to be struggling with somewhat mixed emotions, though she was not going to let the side down. They could see all that in her smile.

'They've found Cop on that island,' said their father, coming straight to the point.

'Is he all right?' asked Lou quickly.

'Very much alive, but not exactly kicking,' said her father. 'They picked him up first thing this morning and flew him straight to Kew Hospital at Invercargill.'

'What about Boozer?' asked Ross, who had forgotten asking the same question in the middle of the night.

'And Ernie?' added Peter.

'Let's see. Boozer first. They rescued him yesterday evening. And you were right, Ross. After a chat with your friend the policeman he soon admitted that Ernie and Cop were on that island. Ernie was flown out this morning with Cop so he's being accommodated by the Invercargill police.'

'Well I hope they treat Boozer okay,' began Ross, but his mother interrupted to reassure him.

'They'll be fair. Don't worry. I'm afraid you'll all have to give evidence. Later on, of course.'

Ross nodded. His mother might be 'afraid', but he reckoned giving evidence would be good fun. Good experience for ... well, it must be good experience for *something*.

'Anyway, Cop seems to want to have a private chat with you kids fairly urgently,' went on their father. 'Could you cope with a three-hour drive? After breakfast, of course. Oh, and your mother's got some clothes for you, I think.'

'New shirts and jeans all round,' said their mother. She took the newspaper from under her husband's arm and opened it. 'Just look at these pictures of you all!'

The three children stood round Cop's bed in hospital. The doctor had given a hopeful report. Apparently Cop had simply been left strapped to the stretcher for those five days. He had been fed at intervals and Ernie had questioned him again and again. Cop had remained silent, pretending it was part of the paralysis caused by his injuries. Then he was left alone. Since movement might have killed him, this was just as well.

Lou, Peter and Ross were telling their adventures again. At last they could mention the map. When they told Cop they had burnt it, he was delighted.

'Splendid idea. Ernie tried to make me draw one for him, but you wouldn't believe how bad that paralysis was. Couldn't move a finger. Not for Ernie, I mean.'

'They didn't realize there were three of us with you,' said Peter.

'I know,' said Cop grimly, 'and I wasn't going to tell them. Not for at least a week. When I got to thinking what the chances were of you ever finding the spot at X and lasting out three weeks till Nick came, well, I began to waver. I think I'd have split on you; there's a limit.'

'There certainly is,' agreed Ross. 'I nearly gave way and told when I heard you weren't in hospital. Then luckily I saw Peter's fire and Boozer stopped asking questions.'

Bit by bit, Cop heard all their adventures. They told him how they had discovered they were actually camping at X. Ross related how he had found out so much from Boozer and then had been trussed up. The marks still showed a little. Peter made an understatement about flying out the helicopter. Meanwhile Lou looked out of the window and realized that the boys had done all the heroics. She had not even found a lake, caught an eel, let alone shot a deer. Just cooked and washed and collected fungi and berries. And yet at the time she had felt brave enough and useful too.

The conversation came back to the mysterious letter X, the unknown quantity.

'You know,' said Peter, his voice betraying the fact that he still felt aggrieved about this, 'we still don't know what we were looking for.'

'Animal, vegetable, mineral?' asked Lou.

'I'll bet we found it,' shrilled Ross. 'We found just about everything. You tell. I bet we found it.'

'Well,' said Cop, 'say it's "animal". What animals did you find?'

Ross had a moment's regret over gold nuggets, but the children started a list of animals with a rush: eels, deer, riflemen, wekas, kakas, bell-birds, tomtits, bush robins, bush canaries, parakeets, grey warblers, blue duck, *sand-flies*, mosquitoes, blowflies ... er ... cockabullies ... um ... moreporks ... oh and glow-worms: the list began to peter out.

'Any good?' asked Ross.

'Not very hopeful, I'm afraid,' said Cop. 'This is something very special. Very rare. Practically extinct.'

'Like the notornis story?' asked Peter. 'People thought those were extinct. But Dr Orbell found them in behind the Te Anau glow-worm caves, still nesting quietly in their old haunts.'

'Do you remember Tepene, the Maori bushman?' asked Cop. 'You met him, Peter. Well, he found one of these creatures. He was afraid for it. But before he died he drew me the first version of our now-famous, non-existent map. He asked me to search for it, telling no one. That was why I didn't tell you. Kind of keeping faith, you know.'

'Gee! you sure that was an ordinary deer I ... I mean we ate?' exclaimed Ross. 'Not a native New Zealand hartebeest or someone-or-other's gazelle?'

'You did mention possums once,' said Peter, secretly kicking himself for ever having resented Cop's keeping X a secret. 'Obviously it's not possums. But if it's of any interest, we didn't, in fact, find any possums.'

'We didn't find any,' said Lou, 'not actually see one. But I think there were some around.'

Cop looked keenly at her.

'Why's that?' he asked.

Peter and Ross made faces at each other. Possums. Two a penny. Why bother with possums?

'There was a place where I picked fuchsia berries that day you two were up the mountain. Just beyond the kaka tree. I saw what looked like possum droppings and sort of chewed-up fern fronds.'

'What was the kaka tree?' asked Cop.

'There was a kaka nesting inside it,' said Lou, 'it was a hollow tree, Ross and I hid in it.'

Cop nodded. Then he said slowly, 'What did the kaka look like?'

'You must know a kaka,' said Peter.

'I do,' said Cop, 'but tell me all the same.'

'Well, it came out at dark,' began Peter.

'It had a fantastic vocab of rude noises,' said Ross.

'It looked like Julius Caesar with no teeth and no chin,' went on Peter.

'Plus sideburns,' added Ross, 'though it's Lou who really saw it, not us. Got your pictures, Lou? Lou drew all sorts of things, Cop. She's jolly good.'

Lou fumbled with the button of her shirt pocket and pulled out the note-book, turned the thin pages.

'Mind the kaka feather,' she said, 'and that powdery wood fell out of its nest. Hang on, I'll put them on the side here on a clean sheet of paper.' She tore a page from the back of the book, arranged the specimens on it and handed the book over to Cop. 'I'm afraid everything's an awful scribble. I meant to look up the plants and ferns when I got home. And birds are specially difficult to draw. Simply won't stay put.'

Cop began turning the pages. He looked very pleased.

'What a marvellous record, Lou,' he said, 'even with the wobbles. These botanical drawings are spot-on for identification. I can name most of them.' He came on the blue duck page. 'Sure about the double call?'

'Absolutely,' said Lou.

'You've got some new stuff in there,' he said, 'you'll have to write it up and publish it.'

Lou laughed. He must be teasing.

Then he came to the kaka pages. Suddenly he was not teasing or joking any more. He began to read out Lou's notes; *'Shriek, boom, glug, click, guggle giggle,'* he read, and Lou began to feel stupid. But Cop went on absolutely seriously: *'Flap, swish, whirr, sailing down like toy aeroplane. Parrot-like. Large hooked bill. Rather stubby wings. Large bird compared with kea? Didn't fly up from ground. Used bill and claws for climbing.'*

Cop stared at the Julius Caesar picture and never even smiled.

'There's another sketch over here,' said Lou, turning the pages. 'I'm afraid I'm no good at birds,' she apologized again.

Cop studied both pictures. Then he put out a hand and touched the powdered wood on the sheet of paper, picked up the feather and examined it very carefully.

'And you found possum-like droppings near here, and chewed fern?'

'Yes,' said Lou.

'Was there any faint sort of path, as though the bird always walked along the same route?'

'Well, yes, there was,' said Lou.

Cop put down the feather. Lou, Peter and Ross could not take their eyes off his face, which looked as though he knew a marvellous secret and was trying to hide it.

'Peter, Ross,' said Cop, 'you found the spot marked X and you diddled Boozer and Ernie. But, Lou' – he turned towards her – 'do you know what *you've* done? Your notes and drawings prove it without any doubt. You've found one of the rarest birds in the whole world. Your kaka isn't a kaka. It's a kakapo, a parrot that's a sort of missing link because it can glide but can't fly. Tepene would want me to tell you now. This is what I was looking for. X stands for kakapo. You found it.'

EPILOGUE

THE children's parents had booked in at a motel, and Lou, Peter and Ross ate an enormous meal and then slept. At visiting time they were back at Cop's bedside.

Peter came straight to the point.

'There's still something we can't understand. Please explain, Cop. Why on earth did Ernie and Boozer want a kakapo and who are Ernie and Boozer anyway?'

'Boozer said it was a ridiculous caper,' said Ross. 'Of course, Boozer's not the bird type.'

'And I don't get why that slinky Ernie went to such risks and expense for a bird,' went on Peter. 'I mean stuffed kakapo aren't hard to come by. Most museums have one, from the early settler days. Live kakapo are so absolutely protected; they couldn't have any re-sale value at all.'

'I don't know,' said Cop listlessly. Lou thought he sounded like a man who had given up all hope of solving the mystery and yet could not stop thinking about it. 'If I'd known anyone was after one I'd've taken more care and certainly kept you three out of it. The only clue I picked up,' he added, 'was one word; Ernie thought I was asleep and I heard him mention "ivory". Doesn't make sense.'

Ross, reacting against Cop's despair, bounced in at once, full of suggestions.

'Simple, my dear Cop, I'll start with Boozer. Did you hear his real name, by the way?'

'Algie,' said Cop dourly. The children's laughter cheered him up a bit.

'Can't call him *that*,' went on Ross, 'but I can reconstruct his life history. It's a simple, sad tale. A helicopter pilot, a nice bloke and then – disaster! He takes to the bottle. Gets struck off the – er –'

'Licence taken away,' said Peter, 'as you said before, for drinking and driving.'

'Yes, that's the story,' went on Ross in a melodramatic voice, 'there he is, a lonely alcoholic and he meets the unscrupulous Ernie, who bribes him with whisky, and ... er ... ivory. Boozer fixes Cop's short shaft and chauffeurs Ernie around as instructed.' Ross dropped his stage voice and went on in all sincerity. 'Poor old Boozer. Maybe he knew Tepene too, in the good old days. Maybe he guessed Tepene'd tell Cop his secret. Everyone knows everyone's business in a place like this.'

Peter began to join in.

'Ernie's name is really Ernst or Ernanini – anyway, something Boozer can't pronounce. Not "one of us" as Boozer said. A foreigner with an accent Boozer can't always understand. Could you place it, Cop?'

'No,' said Cop. 'Not Italian. But something like it. I'm no expert.'

Lou was thinking of the only time she had seen Ernie and of the stunning impression he had made on her. His panache and power. Matadors and millionaires. Those fabulous clothes.

She interrupted her brothers.

'He's from South America,' she said, 'that's my guess. Spanish or Portuguese. He's very rich. Those clothes cost a fortune.'

The boys stared at her.

'Preferred Boozer's get-up myself,' said Ross. 'However our fashion expert reports –'

Cop cut in.

'Spanish or Portuguese. Yes. And certainly no expense spared at that base camp. I think you're on the track. You're very perceptive, Lou.'

Lou shuffled her feet modestly.

169

'Well I just know how I'd draw him,' she went on. 'Binoculars to his eyes and beautifully – well, poised. Not kinked in the back like' – she was going to say 'Peter' but changed this politely – 'like Boozer. He was so relaxed, he'd have watched those parakeets for hours without a crick in the neck.'

'Parakeets?' said Ross. 'I'm not a bird man myself but – parakeets and kakapo. Parrot family. And South American forests are simply squawking with parrots of every hue. So I've read. Don't see what parrots've got to do with ivory. Is there an ivory-crested parrot?'

Peter was suddenly inspired.

'Not *ivory*! That's not what you heard, Cop. Ernie's English isn't too good. He said *aviary*. If he's got an aviary, he'll have live birds in his collection. A collection of every single member of the parrot family.'

'Except this one,' cried Lou, 'the only parrot he hasn't got. I think I can understand in a way. Wanting terribly to make a collection absolutely perfect and complete.'

Ross agreed with that.

'Like my stamps,' he said with a sigh. 'My New Zealand collection'll never be complete. I'll never have a full set of the N.Z. Arms definitives, even if I *do* get a Blue Boy. Too expensive.'

'But nothing's too expensive for Ernie,' said Cop, his voice ringing with enthusiasm. 'You're right. I'm sure you are. The man's obsessed. It's all making sense at last.'

'Well, then,' said Peter, 'there's only one more thing to do, isn't there?'

'First Cop gets fit,' said Lou.

'And then' – Ross was bouncing with excitement – 'then we'll all go back to X. Promise you'll take us, Cop? Back to where X marks the spot?'

INDEX OF MAORI WORDS

haka   = *war dance or challenge*
hu-hu   = *a kind of beetle, with edible grub*
kahikatea   = *native white pine tree*
kaka   = *bush parrot*
kakapo   = *ground parrot*
kea   = *mountain parrot*
kiwi   = *flightless bird*
morepork   = *bush owl*
ngaio   = *native tree*
tui   = *parson bird*
tutu   = *native poisonous tree or shrub*
weka   = *flightless wood-hen*

Some other Puffins

TAKE THE LONG PATH
Joan de Hamel

'I'm not Maori,' said David, but he had spent so much time with his friend Hemi and the old Maori whom he'd met in the cave that he was beginning to believe their stories of ghosts and spirits returning from the dead. Only gradually did he discover he had a special part to play in settling these restless ghosts.

UNDER THE MOUNTAIN
Maurice Gee

Rachel and Theo Matheson are twins. Apart from both having red hair, there is nothing remarkable about them – or so they think. Imagine their horror, then, when they discover that only they can save the world from dominance by strange, powerful creatures who are waking from a spellbound sleep of thousands of years . . .

THE SHADOW GUESTS
Joan Aiken

The deep mystery that surrounded the disappearance of Cosmo's mother and elder brother had never been solved. Then peculiar things began to happen to Cosmo at the old mill house where he was staying. Strangers appeared and only Cosmo could see them. What did they want? Where, or *when*, did they come from?

Heard about the Puffin Club?

... it's a way of finding out more about Puffin books and authors, of winning prizes (in competitions), sharing jokes, a secret code, and perhaps seeing your name in print! When you join you get a copy of our magazine, *Puffin Post*, sent to you four times a year, a badge and a membership book.

For details of subscription and an application form, send a stamped addressed envelope to:

The Puffin Club Dept A
Penguin Books Limited
Bath Road
Harmondsworth
Middlesex UB7 0DA

and if you live in Australia, please write to:

The Australian Puffin Club
Penguin Books Australia Limittd
P.O. Box 257
Ringwood
Victoria 3134